Moon
People

Moon

People

The Age of Aquarius

By

Dale M. Courtney

To order additional copies of this book, contact:
Xlibris Corporation
1-888-795-4274
www.Xlibris.com
Orders@Xlibris.com
49194

Dedication

I would like to dedicate this book to my children. Whom I will always love no matter what. You can do anything you want to in this life, all you have to do is have the will and make it happen.

Moon People

This story focuses on one man by the name of David Braymer and his adventures as 1st Science Officer on the Lunar Base 1 mobile base station. One of three. This book is based on the turning point for Earth into a new era of space travel and the beginning of the "Age of Aquarius". David also has a romance with one of the locals in New Smyrna Beach, Fla. Her name is Cheral Baskel a local restaurant owner. Now during David's experiences he encounters some alien life forms some friendly some not so friendly throughout the universe. David also experiences the space battle of all battles and saves Earth and our new friends. We start our story in the year 2048 when Earth has an aggressive space program. They have just completed two large mobile base stations called Lunar Base 1, 2, and are almost finished with the third base station called Lunar Base 3. They are two miles long and one mile in diameter. They also have one very big surprise. All three ships split into three independent working sections. In addition, all three sections have lasers and rockets and their own engine. They also have shields that are a liquid that turns into a solid mass as hard as 4 inches of steel. When exposed to the cold of space. They also have a couple of lounges where everyone goes for fun. Now on their missions they encounter some new friends called the Powleens. They are very friendly and eventually they join Earth and save Earth together. The Powleens are very tall about seven feet to eight feet on average their legs and arms and torso are elongated also their neck. However, they are humanoid and angels from heaven to Earth.

When the Powleens arch enemy the Arcons find them it is not to good for Earth because Earth is caught in the middle. Well one thing leads to another and before you know it, it is an all out space battle for their existence. I hope you will enjoy it because its action pact from the beginning to the end. Also, keep an eye out for its sequel called Moon People 2, "Mars Reborn". Thank you for your time and may God bless your life.

Sincerely
Dale M. Courtney

Table of Contents

The Beginning
of
The End

Chapter 1

This Story Begins on a beautiful sunny day in Daytona Beach Florida with a man by the name of David Braymer. A 45-year-old single man that works at the local high school as a science teacher. He also teaches astronomy in the 12-grade level. Now he has been here about 5 years and has become somewhat partial to a young lady by the name of Cheral Baskel a local restaurant owner in Daytona Beach Florida. At the moment, Cheral is preparing her restaurant for another shuttle launch at the cape. Everyone always gathers at her place because you can see the launch real good there. It is on the water and its real close to the Cape. She always decks the place out right before a launch too. Now David always goes to Cheral's place before work every morning for breakfast because it is on his way to his school. He has never missed a shuttle launch at Cheral's place since he's been at his school. David was not always a teacher. Before he was a teacher, he use to work for the government for U.F.O. research about five years ago. He didn't like the job that much because he was always bored.

He really wanted to teach anyway. Today is also Oct.27 in the year 2048. The next shuttle launch at the Cape is on Halloween. There has been some unusual events the last 2 shuttle launches though.

They would get right up to the launch sequence and stop the launch for some kind of weird problem.

Now everyone is very suspicious about the next launch on the 31 because of it being Halloween. They have also been launching three shuttles a week. Most of the people going back and forth on the shuttles are workers working on the three huge mobile base stations orbiting the Earth. Two of which are just about finished. They have also been trying to get David to join the crew on the U.S.S. Lunar Base 1 for about 2 years. Which is one of the base stations that is almost completed? However, he declines gracefully because he's a little scared of the launch process, Plus he likes the school he's at. Everybody laugh's about the way the base stations look. They look like a giant empty toilet paper holder from Earth, with one huge engine on the back of it. From in front of the engine to the front of the base station on the inside are all docking bays. There's ten stories' from top to bottom and all three base stations are a mile in diameter and about 2 miles long. They constantly rotate when they are in operation. The U.S.S. Lunar Base (1) and (2) are rotating at this time, and in about 3 months Lunar Base (3) will start rotating. The reason why they want David is his knowledge of the stars. Also because he worked for U.F.O. research.

They pay the workers a lot of money to work on the base stations and he would be an officer if he did decide to join the U.S.S. Lunar Base (1). First it starts on its mission to Mars for 6 months. Then off to Saturn's Moon Titan. The U.S.S. Lunar Base. (2) Will first go to Venus for a year. Then it will head to Pluto and its moon's. U.S.S. Lunar Base (3) will go first to Jupiter for a year and then go to the outer parts of our solar system and beyond. They are also paying big money to either go to our Moon base and our Mar's base to work for a ten year period. Now on this day David is on his way to the restaurant like always listening to his radio. His favorite song is playing when there's a interruption in the broadcast on the Emergency Broadcast System this is K92 FM we take you live to NASA with a special report. This is Steve Slader live on channel 9. Ladies and gentleman today NASA observatory has spotted a huge meteor headed toward Earth at a high rate of speed.

Coming very close. However, NASA officials believe that it will not hit Earth. It appears to be the size of a small Moon. They are also concerned about it hitting the Sun or our Moon. They believe if it hits any other planet we should be all right but NASA experts need to do some more studies and urge everyone not to panic. We're not sure about anything yet. What we do know is, it's coming from the direction of the constellation of Scorpio at the tail area, heading this way going approximately 60'000 miles an hour and it is a planet killer! We repeat please do not panic, now we resume to your regular programming. David was thinking to himself. Oh my God, this is unbelievable. I can't believe this! Could this be the end of us all that everyone predicted? I wonder if Cheral heard it on the news at the restaurant.

As David pulls in to Cheral's place, he sees many of the regular locals parked in the parking lot like normal. As he gets out of the car, he also notices everyone inside looks normal. As he comes through the door Cheral comes over with a big smile on her face. Hi stranger, as she looks at David's face she realizes something is wrong. Then Cheral says, you look like you've just seen a ghost. What's wrong?

David took the worried look off of his face and answered, you haven't heard the news yet have you? No Cheral replied, I just got done in the kitchen and came out and seen you. Why what's wrong? Then David said, it's really nothing to panic about. Well, I just heard something on the radio just minutes ago. They said that there was a big meteor coming right at us from the constellation of Scorpio. Yeah sure that's real funny, Ha Ha. Then David said, no really Cheral I'm not kidding! Turn on your TV. There should be something on there now. I'll bet it's on every station. Cheral looks at David kind of funny and looks over at one of her regulars sitting by the TV and said bill can you turn on the TV that's behind you for me? Bill answered, sure for you anything. Then Cheral said could you put it on channel 9 please? Sure Bill answered. Then on came the TV.

The reporter Steve Slader was talking about the meteor. NASA reports were saying the meteor is increasing in speed. It appears that the meteor is going 69,000 miles an hour and is climbing in speed at the rate of 1,000 miles an hour every 6 hours. This is Steve Slader. I take you live to NASA observatory to talk to Herbert Larson head astronomer. (Herbert Larson) At approximately 3:55 AM this morning we spotted a giant meteor in the constellation of Scorpio coming in our direction. At the current rate of speed, it should be here in about 178 Days.

Now we believe it's going to miss us by about 25000 miles. It's going to be real close, we will be following it very closely. We have experts on this all over the world. Everyone right now is busy trying to calculate where the meteor is going and if it will hit us when it arrives, for the next 178 days. Lady's and gentleman hopefully with God's help nothing will go wrong and we will see the most spectacular event the world has ever seen since the beginning of time. We will be giving you more information as soon as we know more. Please it's very important not to panic it won't help at all. It will only make things worse.

Now we take you back to your regular programming. Now when David came in before everyone knew, it sounded like a regular restaurant with regular restaurant noises. As the reporter started telling everyone what was going on you could hear a mouse burp. Then at the end of the report you heard everyone say the same three words, " Oh my God". About half the people immediately got up with a terrified look on their face and said we have to go, and they paid their tab and left. Then one of Cheral's regular customers in the other half said I'm not going to panic. Hell, it might not even come close to us. Then David said, it would probably collide with something way before it comes near us. I'm going to go ahead and eat. I'm not going to panic either. Then everyone realized who David was and what he did for a living. Then everyone started to calm down and listened to what he was saying. Suddenly everybody went ahead and ate their breakfast. David turned to Cheral with a smile and Cheral said 222? David said you know me, yes maam. Coming right up Cheral replied. She had a sexy smile on her face and then went to the kitchen. David grabbed the newspaper and sat down at his usual booth and started reading the paper.

In no time, one of Cheral's waitresses came out with his breakfast. David ate pretty quickly. He put five dollars on the table and went over to the door of Cheral's kitchen and smiled.

He looked at Cheral and said, that was one good breakfast. That was sure quick Cheral replied. Then David said, yeah I know. You know what? I've been coming here for a long time and you know we never really got to know each other that well.

Do you think maybe that, David seemed to be a little nervous? Well I was wondering if you would like to go out with me some time? Cheral put a sexy smile on her face and said, you know I would really like that a lot. David put a big smile on his face. That's great how about Friday night? Cheral said, ok that sounds good to me. Super David answered. I'll see you on Friday then. He said bye and went on to school. As he was driving to work he notice everyone seem to be driving a little crazy and yelling at each other. When he got to school, he notice everyone was running around panicking. Everybody was telling everyone to calm down. When he got to his room and got settled in. A couple of his best students Billy Berenson and Cathy Rigby arrived. They were a little panicked and asked David, Mr.

Braymer did you hear the news? Sure David replied. I'm going to hook up my new telescope and we will all watch it as it gets close. This is a special telescope that can see during the day.

It is one of the latest telescopes out. Their expensive but they work well. You can hook it up to your computer and watch it on your monitor. With our new chalk board size class computer monitors, we can watch it real good in the classroom, and its high definition too. All you need is the correct coordinates. Then Billy said, that's pretty cool professor. Yeah that is cool Cathy replied!

David spoke up and said I've got to go to the office to get some forms. I will be right back so be good. Billy and Cathy both said, O.k. Mr. Braymer. As David arrived at the office.

Everyone was very busy and a little panicky. It was close to chaos. He went over to the principal's office and walked in. The principal Mike Lever looked at David an said I'm glad you're here. I just received a phone call this morning from NASA. Asking about you and wanting to talk to you. They said it was pretty important. They gave me a number for you to call. I tried to find out what it was about but he wouldn't tell me. I'll bet it has something to do with the meteor doesn't it? I don't know David answered. I'll call and find out and let you know.

David went ahead and got his forms and went back to class. When he got back most of his students were starting to arrive. Everyone was kind of loud so he told everyone to calm down and please sit down. Everyone start studying his or her books for Friday's test I have to make a phone call and I'll be right back. David went to the teachers break room and called the number. Hello, NASA operations Bud Walker speaking. Yes how are you doing, my name is David Braymer, I am a 12th grade teacher at New Smyrna Beach High School. I was told someone was wanting to talk to me and that it was important.

The New Job

Chapter 2

Yes, Mr. Braymer, I'm head of operations out here at NASA. I was wondering if you were still active in the field of astronomy? Yes, David answered.

This is about the meteor isn't it? Yes Bud replied, I hear you're the best at what you do. David smiled and said, well I don't know about being the best. But I do teach astronomy in high school and I have been into astrology for about 20 years. Then Bud said, yes I know Mr. Braymer. Well I'm just going to come right out with it. Our head astronomer Herbert Lawson and his assistant were in a automobile accident yesterday. They're both in pretty bad shape. They will be all right but that gave us some empty positions we have to fill immediately. Because of our meteor that's coming right at us the last calculation shows and there's something else. Then David said, wait I have a job! Yes, I know Bud replied. We are willing to go the extra mile here. We will pay top dollar on this one and we have a substitute to take your place at school. All this is coming straight from the top. Mr. Braymer we need you real bad. We will also help you out with any other problem you might have.

David answered, well I don't know. I guess it all depends on one thing. Then Bud said, what's that? What was that something else you were talking about a minute ago, when you were talking about the meteor? You said there was something else. I can't tell you until you take the job, Bud replied. Then David said, can I have a little time to think about it first? Bud answered, Yes, you have until 5 o'clock today. David said, wow that's not much time. Yes I know Bud said, we can't help it the meteor isn't giving us much choice. Please all I ask is for you to think about it and give me a call later today. Ok sir I'll do that David answered. I'll give you a call either way Mr. Walker and then David said have a good day sir. Then David hung up and went back to class. When he arrived back to class he notice that half of his class was absent and the other half was playing around. All right, everyone sit down, David said. Let's get class going. Billy spoke up and said, does this mean we don't have to come to school because of the meteor. No, you should come to class unless someone says not to, David said. Then Cathy said no one else is. I know but we should still come unless they say otherwise, David replied. Now everyone open their astronomy books to page 286 to the constellation of Scorpio. This is what we are going to study for a couple of days. We will have a test on this Friday. I will also hook this telescope up to our new 80 inch chalk board computer monitor. This ought to be pretty cool once we set it up. Then everyone started studying and David started putting it all together. After about 30 minutes he had it all hooked up and was starting to turn everything on. Suddenly the monitor came on. David started adjusting the telescope to the constellation Scorpio and finally it came in so good it seemed like it was night.

The hole class made a wow sound and then they all said about the same time" cool". At that point David knew he had a hit, then he told Billy to turn out the class room lights. They could see the meteor as clear as night time also everyone shouted out there it is, wow! Look at that picture. David said that's pretty good high definition. It's so clear. The whole class at the same time said yeah! The meteor was coming from the end of the tail section. Where the stinger is in the constellation of Scorpio.

Then Cathy said, Mr. Braymer how's the high definition come in so good, its broad daylight? This is one of the latest telescopes out David said, when you use it in the daytime it mixes with our Hubble 7 satellite telescope in space. That's how it zooms in so close and so clear. That is a good picture, and it looks so close. This is better than I thought! Wait a minute that's not coming from Lambda Scorpio off the stinger that's coming from An tares region but that's over 135 million light years away, there's no way that could get here in one hundred and seventy eight days. I wonder who did the calculations on that?

Boy they do need help! Wait a minute. I should be able to calculate the speed thanks to my new telescope called Zeus. Then David said, Zeus can you locate and lock in on the meteor that is moving told us at a high rate of speed in the constellation of Scorpio? (Zeus) Affirmative, "Located." Cool, the whole class said out loud again. You could see Zeus zoom in on the meteor. Then David said, Zeus can you calculate the speed and size of the meteor coming from the An tares star system, coming to our solar system? Affirmative, one moment please. Meteor is coming approximately 182,000 kilometers an hour and increasing speed 5,005 kilometers every 24 hours. Meteor is ten kilometers in diameter. Wow the class sounded out!

David asked, Zeus how long before the meteor enters our solar system? (Zeus) Meteor will be entering into your solar system in approximately 204 days 6 hours 22 minutes and 44 seconds. Wow the class sounded out! Billy looks at David and yelled out, ask Zeus if the meteor is going to hit Earth. David thought about it for a moment and said maybe I shouldn't. The whole class yells out, why not? Billy tells David hey professor we are all in this together. It's not that simple Billy, David replied. The computer could be off. I just hooked it up.

The Unknown

Chapter 3

There's a lot of things that could be wrong and everyone would leave here and go start a panic all over the place. Billy said, Ah we won't tell anyone. I don't think I can take that chance David replied. Then Billy said, how about if we all pledge not to say anything? David smiled and thought for a moment and said, this is serious people, a lot of people can die in a panic. We will really give our word Billy said, won't we class? Yeah the class sounded out! David laughed and said, ok listen very carefully class. If you here by pledge to this class and to God that you will not tell anyone what we find out in this class about the meteor. I will ask Zeus that question. Everyone has to say I do though. Everybody in the class sounded out, I do. I hope I'm not making a big mistake? Ok Zeus will this meteor collide with any planet in our solar system? (Computer) Negative. There is a 94% possibility that it will collide with your star. The whole class went silent. Then David said, remember people I just hooked this up it may not be accurate. Zeus, is there a chance that it won't hit our sun? Affirmative, there is a 6% chance that the meteor won't hit your star. Zeus do a system check. (Zeus) Affirmative. Zeus is now doing a systems check. A 30 second pause. System check complete, Zeus is functioning at 100 % effectiveness.

The class went silent again and then the bell rang. Remember class don't say anything about what you have heard David said, people can die panicking. You took a pledge. Billy answered, don't worry professor we won't say anything. Then David said, ok I am going to trust you then. There's still a big chance that it won't hit anything.

We know Doc, Billy answered. There's a six percent chance. We'll see you later professor. David grinned and said smarty pants, Ok, good bye. Then Billy laughed and walked out with Cathy and finally all the students cleared out of the room, all of which had a doom look on their face. David thought about it for a minute and decided to make the call. Hello Mr. Walker, this is David Braymer. Bud answered, yes how's it going. Well Mr. Braymer what's it going to be. I believe I'm going to take the job David said. That's great Bud replied. Then David said, by the way sir, what were you talking about earlier? I'll tell you when you get here, Bud said. Ok David answered, I'll go ahead and make arrangements here for a substitute and I'll come on down. I will notify the gate that you are coming, Bud replied. Very good sir, David said. I will see you in a little while. Then Bud said, All right, please drive careful. I will see you in a little while. David went ahead and made arrangements at the office for a substitute and then headed out to NASA. When David finally arrived at NASA, he had forgotten how big NASA has gotten in the past few years. David then found Bud walkers office and went in.

As David was walking in, Bud was walking out and almost bumped into each other. Hey, there he is, Bud said. Then David said, I finally made it. Good Bud replied, why don't you join me and I will take you on a tour to operations real quick. Ok David said. Boy NASA is really getting pretty big isn't it? Bud answered, yes every since we started building these base stations NASA has really gotten huge. David asked, Bud what were you talking about on the phone that you couldn't tell me about? Are you ready for this, Bud asked? Yes I am David said. Then Bud said, here goes. We are still checking but it looks like our meteor has changed direction not once but two times in the past two weeks. David asked, what are you saying? You mean you're saying it's a spacecraft? No sir Bud said, I'm only telling you what I know. There's something else. David said what? Bud answered, the meteor was going 64,000 miles an hour and then all of our instruments indicated it increased its speed to double in less than 10 minutes. It's also ten kilometers in diameter. David said, that's incredible. Bud replied, yeah I know I said the same thing. Then David said, so what's everyone speculating? Well it goes from one thing to another, Bud said. One person says maybe the reason that the meteor changed direction was from bumping into some kind of an object in space that we can't see. However, that does not explain the increase in speed. In addition, the other side of the coin is that it is some kind of an alien spaceship. However, what we do know is that it is ten kilometers in size and now on the present course, it is going to hit our sun. Then David said, I tell you though if someone were going to visit us, they would probably set a course for the star in that system. I never thought of that, said Bud. If they are aliens, I wonder what they want with us.

David told Bud, you know our planet must look pretty good from 135 million light years away. Then Bud said man I tell yeah this meteor sure does look eerie on the telescope. David said, yes I know I have a Zeus telescope system hooked up in my classroom and it practically terrified my class.

It said the same thing yours said. Oh, no, I do not see how we are going to stop a panic if everyone is watching on his or her new telescope, Bud replied.

Then David said, yeah I know what you're saying. Well here we are, Bud said. I would like to introduce you to your new assistant Mr. Kim Moon. How do you do Mr. Moon, David asked? Pretty good Kim replied. I'm a little tired, but I'll be all right. How are you? Mr. Moon Bud said I am putting David Braymer in charge of all operations on the meteor. If you have anything new on the meteor tell this man right here.

The Job Offer

Chapter 4

He is your new boss here on out. David you report to me. Yes sir, David answered. Then Bud said Mr. Moon will you show Mr. Braymer around and update him on everything new? Yes sir, it would be my pleasure replied Kim. Ok good luck, then Bud went back to his office. Kim spoke up and said follow me. I will show you everything there is to know Mr. Braymer. Just call me David. Ok just call me Mr. Moon. No, I'm kidding just call me Kim. Ok Mr. Kim. No just Kim will be fine. Gotcha, David replied. David smiled at Kim, well Mr. Moon what's your assessment of this meteor? Kim looked over at his assistant Martin and said Martin would you put the meteor on the main viewer. Yes, sir answered Martin. Well David said Kim, sir I would have to say at the moment there's not enough data but one thing is for sure we are going to find out because it's coming right at us. In addition, it's ten kilometers wide. Yes, I know, David said.

We were tracking it at our school. This satellite system makes our new system at school look like a toy.

Then Kim said, it should because this is the best telescope system in the world. As they, were both looking at the viewer at the same time? There was a sudden flash of light and the meteor suddenly vanished. What happened, David asked? I do not know, Kim replied. Martin do a system check. I'm on it, Martin answered. Then Kim said, let me check a few things here. I'm just going to zoom in on our friend. Suddenly the screen zoomed in but there was still no sign of the meteor. Did it explode? There were large amounts of radiation all around the area. Kim was asking himself. There doesn't seem to be any debris anywhere, it's as if it just vanished. Well maybe we don't have to worry about the meteor any more. (David) Wow maybe. (Kim) Let's keep after it and do some more studies. Wait did you see that? (David) Yeah, that second flash. Yes, Kim replied, look how far away that was from where the meteor was last reported. Then David said, do you think that was the meteor? Kim answered, I do not know. Let me look at something real quick. Just as I thought. That flash of light was on the same heading as our meteor was on when it disappeared. But in order for it to get to this point, this quick it would have to be doing an excess of about 300,000 miles an hour. Wow, that's incredible! (David) Yeah do you think that's the meteor? That flash of light. (Kim) I don't know it sure does look funny. We will keep watching it. If it flashes again and it's on the same course, we'll know something's up. Then David said, I'm going to inform Bud of what's going on. Sure Kim said. I'm going to do some more checking and I'll get back to you. Ok David replied, I'll use this phone. Bud answered hello. David spoke up Bud, it's me David Braymer. I already have a report to make. It is kind of great news. Then Bud said, oh yeah what is it?

Well it seems our meteor has vanished off the charts in one big flash of light David said. Are you kidding me Bud asked? No, I'm not replied David. We also could not find any debris either. Except large amounts of radiation and there's one more thing. We also seen a flash of light 1 light year away. Three minutes after the meteor vanished. It was on the same heading our meteor was on. (Bud) Wow, all that just happened?

I just left you 5 minutes ago. Man there's all kind of stuff happening today. (David) Yes, I know Kim and I was just watching the big view screen when it happened right in front of us. We are watching to see if there are any more flashes of light even further down the same heading as our meteors heading. (Bud) Why what's everyone speculating? (David) We're not sure yet. Nevertheless, it may be the ends of all of our problems. Then Bud said Boy, wouldn't that be a load off of everybody? Oh yes, David before I go I wanted to talk to you about something very important.

Oh, what's that, David asked? (Bud) Well I just got off the phone with the White House. We've got orders to get these base stations on their way with their missions with a full crew and supplies. I have another Job offer for you. (David) Oh really what's that? (Bud) We need a 1st Science Officer and navigator, and also a astronomer for U.S.S. Lunar Base 1. The pay is excellent. You would have the rank of Captain. You would be under the command of Admiral Benson. Now I know him personally and not only is he pretty sharp. He's also a great guy to work under. However, it is long term. It doesn't get any rawer than this it takes a special kind of man to do something like this but if you have the stones, we've got the job for you. Then David said, this is quite an offer. I've always wanted to do something like this. I was offered this a couple of years ago but I turned it down. I didn't think it was for me. However, I never in a thousand years thought that I ever would do it for real. (Bud) Well think it over. I've got to make a decision quick so let me know within the next couple of days until then, you can run operations on the meteor project.

The Big One

Chapter 5

Keep me informed could yeah. (David) It would be my pleasure sir. (Bud) I'll catch you later. (David) Yes, sir I'll keep you informed and I'll let you know about the job to. Have a good one. David hung up the phone and started to stare at the large monitor. Kim walked over to David and said what did Bud say about the meteor? (David) He couldn't believe it. He also offered me the position of First Science Officer aboard the Lunar Base 1. (Kim) Wow, what did you tell him? (David) That I don't know and I would have to think on it. Hey maybe we shouldn't tell anyone about all this yet, Ok? (Kim) Gauche. I've been watching the monitor and I haven't seen any more flashes. It just seems to have vanished. I also alerted the computer to tell us if there are any more flashes of light anywhere on the heading that our meteor was on before it vanished. (David) Well maybe it is no longer a problem anymore. Nevertheless, we will keep on watching just the same.

You never know any more. Hopefully it will just go down in history as a big scare. Suddenly the phone rings its Bud.

Hey, David I have the press all over me here. I am going to have to tell them something. Have there been any more flashes of light or anything else to talk about? Can we say we are out of danger yet? What do you think? (David) Bud so far we have not seen any other phenomenon in the area and everything looks normal. I have to say it does look like we might be out of the woods. I guess I would tell them that, and that we will keep on watching the area just to be sure but everything at the moment looks great. (Bud) Ok that is what I am going to say then. Hey, don't forget to let me know about that job. (David) You got it. I'll call you in the next 2 days or I'll be here, and I'll let you know. (Bud) All right, I'm going to go ahead and go. I have some stuff I have to get down. I'll see you later. (David) All right, see you tomorrow sir. Hey Kim if you want, let's go ahead and keep and eye on that meteor's heading. If you see another flash give me a call right away. I'm going to go ahead and leave. I have a lot of things to think about and do and very little time to do it in. (Kim) All right I'll see you in the morning. David went ahead and left and went to his house in New Smyrna Beach. When he got there, he made himself a sandwich, sat down, and <u>told his computer to turn on his T.V.</u> There was already a news update on about the meteor disappearing. Everyone seemed like they were back to normal acting again. I wonder if I could just pick up and go? Man being a Captain on a base station would be really cool. There is a ten-year commitment though. Boy that's a long time. All of my students would probably think that it would be cool to have their teacher on a base station. I really don't have anything holding me down here except my class and they could live without me. You know I might just take that job. Bud said the job paid good and I bet it does.

It would sure beat what I'm making now. Maybe I should have taking the job two years ago. Its seems to be my destiny. You know I think I'll eat my sandwich and go to class and get a few things together. I'll take another look at Zeus. All of the students should be gone by now. David ate his sandwich and went back to school.

As he was arriving, everyone was just about gone for the day. He went in his room and turned on Zeus. He focused where the meteor was last sighted. He just started staring into space in deep thought for about 30 minutes.

You know most people live their whole life and never get a chance like this. I do love space and everything in it. I always have. I believe I am going to do it. I think I will take this job. David wrote a good-bye letter to his class and went home. The next morning David got up early and headed straight to Cheral's restaurant. When he got there he sat down at his regular booth. Cheral walked right over and said hey stranger how's it going?

Real good David replied. You're not going to believe what all happened to me yesterday. (Cheral) Oh, what happened? (David) Well yesterday, NASA called me and needed me to help with the meteor so I took the job. Then they went ahead and offered me another job on the U.S.S. Lunar Base 1 as the 1st Science Officer. (Cheral) Wow, are you going to take it?

(David) I do not know. I think I might. I will never get a better offer than this. I always wanted to do something like this but I never thought I would ever get the opportunity. (Cheral) Isn't that a long-term commitment? (David) Yes it is. It's a ten-year commitment. (Cheral) Wow, that is long term. (David) What do you think I should do? (Cheral) I think you should do what your gut is telling you to do.

(David) My gut is telling me to do it. (Cheral) Then I think you should do it. (David) Do you still want to go out with me tomorrow? (Cheral) I wouldn't miss it for the world. Do you want your regular 222 (David) You bet.

The Crew

Chapter 6

David grabbed the paper and ate his breakfast. He told Cheral he would see her tomorrow night at seven and they would go out and eat somewhere. Cheral had a big smile on her face and said, that sounds great. David said I will see you then and went onto work. He finally arrived at operations at NASA and everyone was just changing shifts. Kim was just arriving too and said good morning. (David) Good morning, (Kim) I have already checked, there has not been any more flashes of light last night or our alarm would have went off. I guess we might be out of the woods. (David) I think we are too. (Kim) Well did you decide yet about the job on U.S.S. Lunar Base 1? (David) I think I am going to take it. (Kim) All right, I bet you will love that job. (David) I hope so because it is a ten-year commitment. The only thing I do not like about everything is that my shuttle goes off on October 31, which is Halloween. Kim smiled some and said you know you're right. I never thought of that. I think that would bother me to. (David) I am going to go ahead and call Bud and tell him the good news.

David calls Bud and Bud answers the phone, Hello. (David) Hey, it's me David Braymer, I just wanted to call and tell you that I have decided to take the job on U.S.S. Lunar Base 1. (Bud) Hey, that's great. You know they really need you aboard. You will have a good crew aboard the U.S.S. Lunar Base 1. Well I guess you need to talk to Admiral Benson. I will call him in a couple of minutes and set everything up, and you can talk to him today sometime and you can make arrangements with him. He will probably want you to go and pack what you want to take with you and report to your new home, the Lunar Base 1. Hey, David let me get on this. I will get back to you in a little while. (David) Ok I will catch you later. (Kim) Let me set up the lay out of Lunar Base 1 on the computer and you can check out your new home. It is actually a pretty elaborate space station it has everything on board that a small city has. Including a couple of bars on board and also a couple of shopping malls. A basket Ball court. There is even a small farm on board. You have everything there that you need. You are totally independent. (David) Cool, I will check this out. I might as well get to know my new home. As David went through the Lunar Base 1 program he realized that the base station did have a lot more extras than he thought. It did have everything a city has including a full size hospital and staff. It also has a full size observatory. Which I cannot wait to take a look at. I will bet it is nicer than anything I am use to. Hey, look, here these ships even have weapons. We got a laser and missiles and rockets, wow. She is also very nicely decorated, and very classy looking too. Look here, this baby has got five shuttles also armed with lasers and rockets. All of a sudden, the phone rings. David answers the phone, hello. (Admiral Benson) Hello, Mr. Braymer this is Admiral Benson.

I was just told by Mr. Walker director of NASA that you have decided to take the job of 1st Science Officer aboard the U.S.S. Lunar Base 1. Is that true? (David) Yes, it is. I was hoping I would get to talk to you today about this. (Admiral Benson) Yes as soon as Bud told me about you, I called right away. Two of our crewmembers were hurt in an automobile accident, and we just got orders to leave space dock as soon as possible from the White House. In addition, we are not coming back for a very long time. Are you sure, you want to go? (David) Yes, sir I have made up my mind and there is no turning back now. (Admiral Benson) Ok then welcome aboard. The last shuttle takes off at 0900 0n Monday morning. By the way did you realize that Monday was Halloween. (David) Yes, I know, it does bother me a little bit. (Admiral Benson) You have until then to change your mind. You are going to have to be here a good 24 hours earlier for launch preparations and a quick health check up. Then after that the only thing you are going to see is the stars. Don't worry I'll be there right alongside of you? That's my flight to. (David) Great. The truth about it is I am a little scared of that shuttle launch to the base station especially on Halloween. But I think I will be all right after that. (Admiral Benson) Good Captain Braymer because you and I are going on one hell of a ride Monday morning, trick or treat. I will show you wonders you always dreamed about. (David) That's pretty cool sir. I can't wait. (Admiral Benson) Well then I'll see you around 0900 Sunday for launch preparations. Yes sir David answered. I'll see you then. (Admiral Benson) Ok, good-bye. David hung up the phone. He couldn't believe this was all happening so quick and that Monday morning he was going to leave earth for a very long time.

Kim was watching David and walked over and said, what's a matter you having second thoughts. (David) No not at all. I just can't believe how fast everything in going in my life. (Kim) Yeah I know what you mean. It isn't every day you leave Earth and go out into space. You know Bud offered that other assistant Science Officer job on Lunar Base 1 to me. (David). Hey that's great. Are you going to take it? (Kim) I don't know I'm sure thinking about it. I just might. The pay is great.

Fate Steps In

Chapter 7

That is sure a long time to have to leave Earth. (David) Yes I know, but I've made up my mind and I'm going to do it. (Kim) I wish I could be as sure as you are. (David) I guess I'm ready for a little excitement in my life before I get old and die. You only live once you know. (Kim) Yeah I know what you mean.

I've been here about 10 years and I have gotten use to coming in every day. But I have always wanted to leave on a big space mission. I only have my father to look after. He can take care of himself he don't really need me. Then David said, I'm also doing this because I know I will never get another chance as good as this one, that pays so well with the rank of Captain. You know I feel like I've been giving a second chance in life or live two different lives in two different dimensions. I can't wait to start it. Hey Kim there hasn't been any more flashes of light have there, on the same heading as our meteor was on. (Kim) No sir it looks like we seen the last of our meteor. Everything looks normal in that area of space. (David) You know that sure was weird how that vanished like that. (Kim) Yes I know.

I thought for sure we were going to see another flash of light on down the road on that same heading. I don't know why. I guess it was the way it disappeared. (David) Yes I guess I was kind of hoping that too, but you never really know. You know I've been looking at the U.S.S. Lunar Base 1 on the computer and this base stations got it all just like you said. This little venture may be better than I thought it would be. It's got all kinds of room on it. It says here that it can even come apart in three different independent working sections. In case one or two sections get damaged or destroyed. That's really incredible. I know I'm doing the right thing. Well I'll know if you changed your mind if I see you onboard. You know Kim it's already time to call it a day. Time has really been flying lately. At least it seems that way to me. Hey Kim I'll see you in the morning. Have a good evening. (Kim) You too boss. David went home the whole time he looked like he was in a trance or a state of euphoria.

When he got home he ate a quick sandwich and went to bed. It's like he couldn't wait for tomorrow so he went ahead and went to sleep as fast as he could. The next morning he received a phone call it was Bud. Good morning, how's it going?

(David) Oh pretty good, is everything still on? (Bud) You bet. I just called to tell you not to come in today. Instead take today and Saturday off and get everything in order. You might want to say good-bye to your friends or pack all your stuff you want to take with you. In addition, just bring it with you Sunday morning when you come for launch preparations. (David) Ok, no problem here. (Bud) Ok I will see you Sunday morning then. (David) Ok I will see you then sir.

Then David hung up the phone and got dressed. Well I guess I will go eat some breakfast, go to the school and say goodbye to everybody. Then come home and pack. I guess I will go out to eat with Cheral tonight and then come home and do some more packing. When David arrived at Cheral's restaurant. Everything seemed to be business as usual. Just like it was before the meteor came and went. David sat down in his usual seat and Cheral came out when she seen David come in. Hey stranger how's it going? I've been keeping an eye out looking for you this morning. Are we still on for supper tonight? (David) You bet. I've had nothing else on my mind since we talked about it. I thought we might eat at Red Lobster in Daytona. Wait I don't even know if you like seafood. (Cheral) Don't worry I love seafood and I love Red Lobster, they have great food there. I haven't eaten there in about a year.

This is going to be great. Do you want the usual 222? I would love the 222, thank you. (Cheral) Coming right up. Hey Cindy would you get this man a cup of decafe please. (Cindy) Coming right up, I'll get you a paper too ok. (David) Sure thank you. It didn't take long before Dave's breakfast was done. Cheral brought it out to him and told him that she had one more order to get out and she would come out and sit with him for a while. David said I would really like that, with a big smile on his face. He notice his breakfast was perfect looking. Then he said this breakfast looks good, thank you. Cheral had a big smile and said, any time. David went at it. When he was almost done with his breakfast, Cheral came out and sat down with David. David said this breakfast was delicious, thank you very much. (Cheral) I'm glad you liked it. Did you make up your mind about the base station job? (David) Yes I did. I'm going to do it.

But what I didn't know was that I was going to go so quick. (Cheral) How quick? (David) I have to show up at 0900 Sunday morning for flight preparations and a quick health check up. Then we launch Monday morning on Halloween at 0900. (Cheral) Wow, that is quick.

Saying Good-Bye

Chapter 8

Then David said, by Monday Halloween night I will be sleeping on the base station. (Cheral) Man, that is quick. Then David said, I know, I'm still not use to the idea of that yet. Especially because it's Halloween. (Cheral) You know I just thought about it. You're going to be like Spok on Star Trek. Wasn't he the 1st Science Officer too? David smiled and said yes he was. I never thought of it like that before. You know I was going to eat breakfast and go and say goodbye to my friends at school. Then spend part of the day there and then go out with you tonight. I think I will spend tomorrow packing everything I'm going to need. Then go to NASA for the launch preparations. Wow it sounds like you have it all planed out, replied Cheral. Wait I'm going to get to know you and then you're going to be out of my life. (David) You know you can call me any time you want on my cell phone. (Cheral) Oh really? (David) Yeah and I'll tell you all of the latest news, it will be great. Cheral) All right, that does sound cool. However, it would be better if you were here, so we could go out together though. Although, I guess we all have our destiny or fate we can't avoid. (David) Well you know I hate to leave good company, but I guess I've got to get moving.

I'll see you tonight about 7, is that ok? (Cheral) That's perfect for me. (David) I'll see you then. Goodbye (Cheral) Goodbye. David Left the restaurant and hurried to his school to say goodbye to everyone. When he got there, he went to the office. When everyone saw him, everybody was bomb barding him with all kinds of questions. After conversing a little while he went to his class to say goodbye. When he got their and his class seen him. Everyone stopped what they were doing and jumped up and said hey it's the professor. (David) Hey everybody, sorry to interrupt I just wanted to come by and say goodbye to everyone. Then everyone at once said what, where you going. Billy stood up and said your leaving us. Where you going? Everyone was stunned (David) Well I received an offer I couldn't turn down. Also I tell you honestly I'm going to miss all of you. (Billy) Where you going doc? (David) Well I'm going to be a Captain on the USS Lunar Base 1. All of the class said wow, really? (David) Yes, I'm going to be the 1st Science Officer and I'm going to be gone for a very long time. We're first going to Mars for 6 months and then off to Saturn's moon Titan. There we will be for a very long time unless we get orders to go somewhere else. Then the whole class said wow, that's cool. (Billy) Hey, you're going to be like Spok on Star Trek. (David) Yeah that's what everyone is saying. You know I'm going to periodically call and tell you what we're doing, and about anything that's going on. I'm going to donate Zeus to the class and you can watch us on the monitor here in class. I wanted to come by and say goodbye and get a couple of things. (Billy) Mr. Braymer when are you leaving Earth and going to the base station? (David) I have to be at NASA at 0900 Sunday morning for launch preparations.

Then Monday at 0900 on Halloween my shuttle will take off to the base station. The whole class, it seemed at once said, cool. (Billy) Hey, doc if you need anybody else just let me know, I will go. That would be so cool. (David) David had a big smile on his face and said I do not know if they need anyone else. But if you study hard, you never know. I would be happy to have you aboard, you people go ahead and do what you were doing. I will get a couple of things and be on my way. You know I am going to miss you people and this school. I really liked it here. (Billy) Hey doc, are you scared of the shuttle launch? (David) Yes I sure am. Especially because it will be Halloween. Ok I will go ahead, get my stuff, and be on my way. David got his stuff and said one last goodbye and went home to pack his stuff and then go out on his date. He picked up Cheral and went to Red Lobster and had a great meal and then they went to the beach and parked. (David) You know I have not gone on a date in a long time and you know I am having a great time. (Cheral) I am having a good time too and that dinner was fantastic. I am sorry you are leaving. I wish you did not have to leave so quickly. Yes, I know this is a little over whelming to me too. I still cannot believe I am doing this. (Cheral) I cannot believe it either. Are you sure you don't mind me calling? (David) Not at all. In fact, I'm looking forward to it. Then David looked at Cheral with a serious look on his face and leaned into Cheral and Cheral leaned in and they kissed intently. (Cheral) Wow, what was that? (David) Oh, I'm sorry I shouldn't have done that. (Cheral) No that's all right I really enjoyed it. It's just that I haven't kissed anyone in very long time either and you know I liked it a lot! (David) Would you like me to do it again? Cheral got a big sexy smile on her face and said you know I believe I would. She leaned in toward David and they kissed passionately for about a minute and then stopped.

The Shuttle Launch

Chapter 9

They were both secretly thinking about what they have been missing in their lives. Then David asked Cheral, would you like to come to my place and spend the night? Cheral gave David a funny but sexy look and before David could say, I'm sorry I shouldn't have said that. Cheral said you know I must be crazy but I believe I do and then smiled. David couldn't believe she said yes. He got the biggest smile on his face and kissed her one more time and said this is turning out to be the best night I've had in a very long time. Cheral said me too and they left the beach and went to David's house and they made passionate love for a very long time. The next morning when they woke up. They woke up starring at each other with a big smile on each other's faces and Cheral said I had the best time last night and now you're going to leave me. Then David said, I know before, all I was going to just miss was my students and know I'm going to miss being with you. I haven't been with someone like you in a very long time. I had so much fun with you last night and making love to you was so beautiful.

I will remember it always. Cheral gave another sexy look at David and said you know I don't have to be at the restaurant for a couple of hours. What do you say about going one more time around the world? Then David said that sounds fantastic and leaned over and started kissing Cheral and they made love again. (Cheral) You know David I can call Marsha and see if she can fill in for me today and I can spend the rest of the day with you if you want. David said I would really like that a lot! Then Cheral called Marsha and made arrangements. Then they made love some more and spent the day together. They had a lot of fun and then stayed Saturday night together and they made love most of the night. In fact, when David woke up by the alarm, they were both very tired. They both got dressed and then decided that Cheral could drop off David at NASA. Then take his car home and then take a taxi to the restaurant. When they arrived at NASA. They kissed passionately for about 5 minutes and Cheral started crying and said I'm going to miss making love to you. David started hugging Cheral and said I'm really going to miss making love to you too and most of all being with you. You know it seems like my life is moving so fast that I don't know what to do. But I know the only thing in my life I regret, is leaving you. They kissed one more time and Cheral said I hope you have a safe flight. We will all be cheering for you at the restaurant. Oh and one last thing, you take good care of yourself, your my rocket man. They kissed one last time and Cheral left and David went inside for his launch preparations and his check up. He checked in to Doctor Blues office and took about 20 tests, and was hooked up to a computer with electrodes all over him for about 3 hours. Then Doctor Blues came and passed him on everything. He knew he was healthy though, he had just had a check up. Then he went to watch a video on the launch itself. Then he went to the launch psychotherapist for about 2 hours and finally was sent to his launch quarters and watched a little T.V. Then he went right to sleep that night because he was so tired from making love with Cheral all night. He wasn't even thinking about the shuttle launch until the next morning. But when he woke up Monday morning and put on his new Captains uniform and he looked in the mirror and realized what he was doing. Then they helped him put on his flight suit and got in the shuttle, he was terrified almost at the point of shock. All he kept saying was what did I get myself into. He also kept asking his shuttle Captain, Captain Briggs is everything all right. All the way up to 0855 and Captain Briggs just kept saying all systems are a go. David looked over at Admiral Benson and he looked as calm as a cucumber, then he couldn't say a word the rest of the launch. Then there was lift off. 10, 9, 8, 7, 6, 5, 4, 3, 2, 1 ignition full thrust. David griped the launch chair with the grip of steel. Then as the shuttle started sounding like thunder and a lot of vibration. Captain Briggs said, happy Halloween NASA and we started to move upward it was looking like a perfect launch. (Captain Briggs) NASA we have lift off. All systems are a go.

(NASA) Copy that shuttle Eagle. Your all go, down here. Coarse laid in and all systems look good. (Eagle) Roger that. (NASA) You're on your way Eagle. Have a nice flight. (Eagle) See you on the flip side. (NASA) Roger that. David looked out into space with an awe look of amazement.

The G force was right around 4 G's until they left the Earth's atmosphere. Then David started to relax a little bit, after that it was smooth sailing. As they headed toward the base station, he saw how huge Lunar Base 1 really was. It was 1 mile in diameter and 2 miles long. Everything that he was watching seemed to be like a movie. As they were coming close to Lunar Base 1's docking bay he notice how vast space really looked and how beautiful it was. He got so excited. Then he heard "Shuttle Eagle "this is U.S.S. Lunar Base 1 do you read me?

Happy Halloween

Chapter 10

Roger U.S.S Lunar Base 1, this is Captain Briggs on shuttle Eagle come in. (Captain Williams) Captain we need you to dock at docking bay number 4, over. (Eagle) Roger Lunar Base 1. Locking in computer data now. Now we are on auto. (Captain Williams) Copy shuttle Eagle we will do the rest from here. USS Lunar base 1 out. Docking went as smooth as butter. They made it look so easy. We had to wait about 30 minutes before we could unload off the shuttle. The base station looked like a small city it was so big. Also the lighting in space was awesome. Admiral Benson and I unloaded off the shuttle Eagle and I had to do my first salute to Lieutenant Commander Mark Craft second in command. (David) Captain Braymer reporting for duty sir. (Lieutenant Commander Craft) Welcome aboard sir. (Admiral Benson) Thank you Commander. Permission to come aboard Commander? (Lieutenant Commander Craft) Permission granted sir. Well Captain how did you like the ride here? (David) I don't believe I'll ever forget that lift off sir. (Admiral Benson) Yes I know every time I take a shuttle to here it seems like the first time. I would like to introduce you to Lieutenant Courtney. She will show you to your quarters and show you around.

If you have any questions, you can ask her. We are also going to have a briefing in about four hours, I'll see you there. Lieutenant Courtney will show you where, Ok. Welcome aboard Captain. I have to get up to the bridge so once again welcome to the team. (David) Thank you sir, it's an honor to be here. (Lieutenant Heather Courtney) Captain Braymer if you'll come with me, I'll show you to your quarters. As we walk, I will point out some of the general places like restaurants and shopping facilities where we have anything you would want or be able to get on Earth. We have it all here sir. We are totally self sufficient we even have a huge greenhouse. We have one of the best observatories around. I go there quite often to think. We also have a few lounges on board where everyone gets together and has a lot of fun. (David) This is so impressive! Do we have livestock onboard to or is everything come pre packaged? (Lieutenant Heather Courtney) No sir we were going to have livestock but we realized we really don't need livestock. For instance, we use powdered milks powdered eggs. Some people have pets and we have one private that has a couple of chickens for real eggs but you have to have special permission though. If you notice we have everything categorized with the alphabet like each of the sections on board are A through Z. We also use numerical order. Your quarters are in D section room 101. It's a 1-bedroom apartment layout. Just like any other apartment on Earth and some are very elaborate, yours is like medium to elaborate. We are coming up to your place now. It doesn't look like much from the hallway but once you go in you'll see it's a homey environment just like Earth. Lieutenant Courtney opened the door and as they went in. David noticed how nice his place was and said very nice, this is nicer than my house on Earth.

(Lieutenant Heather Courtney) All of the plumbing is the same on Earth except there are little water pumps in the system to help it along. The waste all goes to an area where the water is separated from the waste and dried and then the waste is taken to the greenhouse to be used as fertilizer. We also use the byproduct of methane gas to make electricity and fuel and many other things on the ship. We have artificial gravity and on a rare occasion we lose it or it's not as accurate as we would like, but were working on that problem. So a lot of stuff is better if they have velcro on it in case we lose gravity. Soon you're going to notice that all the glasses have flip top covers. You always get a cover for your plate just so you don't have one hell of a mess to clean up when you lose gravity. You'll get use to it. Some places you'll notice, have more gravity than others. We have a lot of areas that have no gravity that we can't help. In some areas on the ship you'll see that the gravity is about one half of our normal gravity and it's really fun because you're like superman. You can jump higher and farther and do a lot of crazy stunts, lift heavier objects. We are studying this and we are starting to design new games every day. The gravity thing has got its pro's and con's. Sometimes for instance, you'll be sleeping and you will wake up kind of floating over your bed for a second or two and then fall back on the bed. We've had a few minor injuries all ready but nothing serious yet because everyone is usually asleep on their bed when it happens. That's why we're trying to educate everyone. Most people tuck them self's in a certain way so that doesn't happen. Nevertheless, you will also find that you get a good RM sleep that's like no other. You wake up so rested you fill great and you also do not need as must sleep because of it. Some people get space sickness.

Don't worry we have a fully staffed hospital that has all of the latest advancements. We also have several gyms on board all over the ship. Now Captain they have all of your luggage and they will be bringing it to you in a little while. If you're in the briefing they'll just set it inside of your door. One last thing in your den there is a computer link up to our main computer and in any room in your apartment; you have a telecom system that's also connected to the main computer. All you have to do is say the location or name first to anywhere on the ship and pause. Now when it rings it's the normal standard Navy whistle, but you can change it to any of about a 1,000 different other tones if you wish. Finally, here is your communicator this goes on your uniform. It's a simple on and off switch and exactly like the intercom, it is also connected to the main computer. If you want the computer, all you have to do is push the button and say the word computer first and pause. We even have an Olympic size swimming pool that we also use as a water reservoir. It also has a covered top that is 5 feet above the water that's totally in cased, in case we lose gravity. Now let me see, is there anything that I'm forgetting? (David) Well there sure is a lot of neat stuff on board. I love this. I think I'm going to be really happy. I fill really lucky to be here. You know Lieutenant that has to be one of the best briefings I have ever had! (Lieutenant Heather Courtney) Thank you sir, it's my pleasure. However, believe me sir there is so much more. I'm still learning new stuff every day too. I've been on the ship only about 2 months myself. (David) I do think you forgot one thing though. (Lieutenant Courtney) Oh, what's that sir? (David) I still don't know where the briefing room is. Lieutenant Courtney started laughing and said I'm sorry sir, I forgot to tell you. Its right down the hallway in C 106.

Since you brought that up on your computer under ship access there's a detailed layout of the entire ship sir. (David) Lieutenant I'm going to tell the Admiral that this was the best briefing I have ever had. (Lieutenant Heather Courtney) Thank you sir, if there are any more questions, you can find me on the ships directory any time. (David) Thanks again Lieutenant. You have a good evening. (Lieutenant Courtney) Thank you again sir, just remember there's no such thing as evening in space. David starting smiling and said you know you're right. I'm going to have to look at things totally different now. Goodbye Lieutenant. (Lieutenant Courtney) Goodbye sir. Lieutenant Courtney left and David went into the living area and sat down and notice as he looked around, he had one good size window in his dining area into the heavens. You could see Earth and he noticed how beautiful Earth was. Clearly, you can see from space that the Earth was a gift from God! David just sat there looking out the window in awe. (David) Boy if it looks this good here, I wonder what it looks like in the observatory. All of a sudden, he heard his telecom on his uniform sound off the navy whistle, Captain Braymer this is Lieutenant Courtney, again sorry for bothering you sir, I just wanted to remind you of the briefing in 3 hours. (David) Thank you Lieutenant. I was just sitting here looking out my dining room window in unbelief. (Lieutenant) You know that seems to be the first thing everyone notices when they get here. In fact, I did the very same thing. It literally takes your breath away when you first see it. (David) It sure does. (Lieutenant) Captain you also have time to take a nap and distress before the briefing if you want. Just tell the computer to wake you up at 15 minutes before the briefing in C-106. Also if you need a sleep aid, just tell the clinic.

They will send it to you in your mailbox by your front door. It works on air. Your medicine will arrive in about a half an hour or sooner. (David) Wow, that's service for you. (Lieutenant) We aim to please sir. (David) One last thing, you are doing a great job Lieutenant. (Lieutenant) Thanks again sir. I'll see you in the briefing sir, goodbye (David) Goodbye again Lieutenant. A nap might be a good Idea. Well let's go check out the bedroom. David went over and opened the door to his new bedroom and he liked it, it was very elaborate. It had all kind of extras. He laid down on his bed and it was the most comfortable bed he had ever laid on. This isn't that bad at all. I'm going to love this job. Computer. (Computer) Working! (David) Wake me up at 0345. (Computer) Affirmative. Then in a matter of minutes he fell asleep. David slept so deep he didn't wake until the alarm went off. (David) Computer (Computer) Working. (David) Computer turn off the Alarm. (Computer) Affirmative. David jumped up and straightened out his uniform and got a drink of water and hurried down the hall to the briefing room. When he got there, everyone was starting to arrive. He went ahead and found a seat and waited for everyone to arrive. There were about one hundred people. Finally, the Admiral came right at 0400. Admiral Benson walked right over to the podium and started addressing everyone. Ladies and gentleman, my name is Admiral Benson for some of you who don't know me. I'm your commanding officer here on Lunar Base 1.

Status Quo

Chapter II

I want to thank all of you for coming and to tell everyone what a great job you doing. I know we have all been working hard to get everything ready to embark on our mission. Now we have received more orders to launch on our mission as soon as tomorrow morning at 0800 hours. Lunar Base 2 has orders to leave the day after tomorrow at the same time. I can't tell you how important this is. We all have to check and double check every little thing to make sure we're not over looking anything because once we leave we're not coming back for a very long time. However, we will still have supply ships every now and then with some more people coming but other than that we are on our way to Mars. Right now, we are doing fine. We are on schedule and everything is a go. I want to welcome our new 1st Science Officer Captain Braymer aboard. Where you at Captain? (David) I'm here sir. David stood up. (Admiral Benson) There he is.

Welcome aboard Captain. (David) Thank you sir, glad to be here Admiral. (Admiral Benson) You can go ahead and sit back down Captain. David sat back down. If anyone has any science questions, you can go to Captain Braymer. Captain I will see you on the bridge at 0600 tomorrow morning (David) Yes sir. (Admiral Benson). Now we have approximately less than 16 hours before we shove off. I suggest we make them count. Now if anyone is having second thoughts about going, tell me know or forever hold your peace. No one said anything. Then the Admiral said, Thank you, everyone is dismissed. Now as everyone was leaving Admiral Benson walked over to Captain Braymer. Well Captain how do you like you quarters. (David) I love it sir. And that view from my window is breath taking. (Admiral Benson) I know Captain I still can't get over being up here too. If you have, any problems don't hesitate to tell me. I will see you at 0600 on the bridge tomorrow. (David) Yes sir. Then Admiral Benson went back to the bridge and David went back to his quarters. He watched a little T.V. and told the computer to wake him at 0500 and went to sleep. At 0500, David got up, got dressed quickly and said I have to look and see where the bridge is on the computer. He hurried out the bedroom door and seen the dining room window and that incredible view and it seem to stun him again. He went into the kitchen and he noticed a large what looked like a microwave oven with instructions next to it. The instructions said to call the kitchen and tell them what you want. Then they will send it to you through an air tube, which runs on a air system like the mailbox and then you warm it up in the microwave. Also he looked over on the counter and he noticed a good size menu. He looks through the menu for a minute and decides to try an order.

(David) Here goes. He depresses the button on his uniform and pauses, to tryout his COM. (Computer) Working. (David) Computer, I would like a cup of coffee and 2 fried eggs over easy with 2 pieces of bacon and also two pieces of rye toast. Also in my coffee, I would like two tablespoons of sugar and a little cream. (Computer) Affirmative. Please allow two minutes. (David) Wow, that's pretty easy, and just like the computer said it came in 2 minutes exactly. David went ahead and ate his breakfast and heads to the bridge. He arrives at the bridge a little early. The first person he sees is Lieutenant Commander Robert Tice head of security. Hello sir, good to have you aboard. (David) Hello Commander my name is. Before he could get the words out Commander Tice said your name is Captain Braymer 1st Science Officer of our Lunar Base 1 ship sir. (David) Very good Commander. What would you have me call you. (Commander Tice) Either Commander Tice or Robert and some call me Bob. On the bridge sir most of the time we are informal unless things get serious. (David) Gotcha Commander. (Commander Tice) Sir this is your station area over here. The Commander pointed to a rather large custom console type of desk with many LED displayed lights all over it with a couple of dials and levers and couple of view screens and three large reclinable chairs with what looked like a race car drivers shoulder strap seat belts that attach to the back of the chair when not in use. There were many chairs like this all over a pretty good size bridge and one that stood out over all the others. That had to be the Admirals chair. In front of the bridge, was a large view screen kind of looked like a movie theater room? Then suddenly the door to the bridge opened and it was the Admiral. (David) Hello sir. (Admiral Benson) Hello, Captain how do you like the bridge? (David) Very impressive sir. I particularly like my area Admiral. Then the door opened again and there was about eight people coming in. Three women and five men. Everyone saying hello to each other, and then saying hello to the Admiral, and then going to the stations. (Admiral Benson) Hello, everybody glad to have you aboard. I would like those who are not familiar with their area too please do so. We have about one hour before we launch. Sorry to rush you but it can't be helped.

The Mission Launch

Chapter 12

We have our orders. Everyone started familiarizing themselves with their area. David was fascinated with all the latest instruments on his console. He had a view screen that was connected to their observatory computer and a new radio waves emissions meter that was so actuate that you could detect if a planet had water or land or oxygen and what gases there was on the planet or moon. He also had a long distance sound emitter that could pick up sounds from great distances away. He was not familiar with many other instruments. Now among there crew was Lieutenant Tawny Fisher who was our pilot and next to her was Jenna Parsons who was are copilot and navigator. Also there was the Admirals right hand man Lieutenant Commander Mark Craft second in command on board. Our Communications Officer was Lieutenant Charles Courtney brother of Heather Courtney. Lieutenant Charles Courtney spoke seven different languages but his computer could speak over one hundred languages. It looked like we had a great crew. Now we were all busy familiarizing ourselves with our stations when the time for our launch was approaching. Then all of the sudden the Admiral spoke to his intercom over the entire ship. Hello men and women aboard the U.S.S. Lunar Base 1. We are about to embark on a historical journey out into our solar system to Mars first and then to one of Saturn's moons Titan and then beyond. We have in my opinion the best crew in space. So try not to worry. We have orders to launch at 0800 and we are functioning at 92%. The other 8% are things that are unrelated to ships function. Mainly stuff we haven't unpacked yet.

It's 0745 and in 15 minutes, we are going to launch. Before that I will tell you on the intercom to secure yourself in one of many locations on the ship by telling you red or yellow alert if you do not know your location please ask a supervisor in any area. You should always secure yourself in your chairs with your harnesses latched. When we say red alert you should preferably be at your location or post when we say yellow alert it means to go immediately to your stations and prepare for a red alert. We will start the countdown at T minus 10 minutes and counting. Thank you for your cooperation. Five minutes later the Admiral went on the intercom again and said, this is Admiral Benson, we are now going to yellow alert. I repeat yellow alert. Then you could see a yellow light blinking in every room. You could also hear the Navy whistle sound off over and over for 5 seconds. Then it was just the yellow light blinking in the room. Also a few minutes later you could hear the Admiral say, this is Admiral Benson we are now going into red alert. I repeat this is a red alert. Prepare for launch.

Then the Admiral said we are now going to begin our launch sequence at T minus 10 minutes and counting starting now. Mark T minus ten minutes and counting. Then the LED display on the wall started the countdown. Lieutenant Fisher it is time to warm up our engine. Remember everyone please get buckled in at your stations. (Lieutenant Fisher) Yes sir. Lieutenant Fisher turned on the engine and started to warm it up. It was T minus four minutes 23 seconds and counting. Then it got down to T minus 43 seconds (Admiral Benson) Lieutenant Parsons how's everything looking. (Lieutenant Parsons) Were looking good sir, all systems are a go. In addition, the course is laid in sir. Then it got down to T minus 15 seconds and counting. Then 10, 9, 8, 7, 6, 5, 4, 3, 2, 1 ignition full thrust. Suddenly the ship started to vibrate just a little and then we started to move. It wasn't that bad. Everyone started cheering and clapping. (Admiral Benson) Lieutenant Fisher let's start out on impulse and then we'll go to Mock 5. (Lieutenant Fisher) Affirmative sir. (Admiral Benson) How's everything looking Lieutenant Parsons? Let's gradually build up to mock five. (Lieutenant Parsons) Yes sir. We're looking good sir, all systems are a go, and we're on coarse too sir. (Admiral Benson) Well there's no turning back now. We are on our way. Then everyone cheered again. A few hours had past and the Admiral asked Lieutenant Parsons again. How are we looking now Lieutenant Parsons? (Lieutenant Parsons) All systems are looking good sir. (Admiral Benson) Lieutenant you let me know if there are any changes and let whoever takes your place at shift change know the same thing. I want to know anything out of the ordinary. I'm going to my quarters. Commander Craft you've got the helm. She's your bridge now.

(Commander Craft) Yes sir. Those of you who are not connected to the running of the ship can stay or leave at your own will if not sure, ask permission. The Admiral was gone for about a half of an hour. Then all of the sudden Lieutenant Courtney said to the Commander sir, we are getting an incoming communiqué from NASA. Then Commander Craft said oh really patch them through to my COM Lieutenant. (NASA) Commander Craft this is Kim Moon here at NASA. We just wanted to say that was a picture perfect launch. Congratulation. (Commander Craft) Thank you Mr. Moon we're on top of the world up here to. (Kim) That's not all I called about Commander. (Commander Craft) Oh really what's up. (Kim) Well sir we have just spotted a large explosion a few light years from our solar system. We can't tell what happened but it was bright. It was on the same heading that our meteor was on when it disappeared. I told Captain Braymer I would contact him if there was another flash of light on that same heading. But we don't see how it could be our meteor because it traveled to far across the galaxy and too fast to be our meteor sir. (Commander Craft) Is there any debris coming this way? (Kim) No sir, there's no debris at all Commander, that we can see, just like before. But it is on that exact heading the meteor was on. I'm going to patch you through to Captain Braymer. Lieutenant Courtney give Captain Braymer this call. (Lieutenant Courtney) Yes sir. (Captain Braymer) Hello, this is Captain Braymer. (Kim) Hello Captain this is Kim Moon at NASA how do you like your new job? (David) I love it. I'm just getting situated. (Kim) I don't know if you've seen it yet but we had another flash of light on that same heading. (David) Oh really. Where at? (Kim) About 2 light years from our solar system.

(David) You're kidding? (Kim) No sir I'm not. Was there any debris? (Kim) No, none just like before. There's not a trace of anything that we can see, except a lot of radiation. (David) Well, there's no way that could be our boy could it? It was 135 million light years away from us. That was too far away. (Kim) Yeah that's what I thought too. I just wanted to tell you so you could watch it too. I knew you wanted to know if we seen any more flashes of light and I wanted to see how you liked it up there. (David) I tell you Kim it's unbelievable up here. It's like being in a movie. And the view is incredible. (Kim) Man, I wish I were up there with you. (David) You can still change your mind and join us. (Kim) No, my place is down here with my feet firmly on the ground. (David) Suit yourself, but I have made up my mind. I love it. (Kim) You take good care of yourself and I'll catch you later. (David) You too, goodbye Kim. David was happy because he was getting ready to use his new telescope equipment. As he got his station active he started doing some tests on the location that Kim gave him, where they seen the flash of light. He was either looking for debris or watching for another flash of light or anything that was abnormal. He was also checking for any type of gases with his new radio waves emission meter. And this observatory telescope had the capability of zooming in and isolating a certain area in a one-mile radius, millions of light years away. David noticed there was some reminisces of gases. He started to try to isolate and identify each gas to attempt to discover what type of explosion it was. Hey there's high levels of radiation here. That must have been a massive explosion. But what the hell did it? That's so strange, there is no debris. What exploded? This is illogical. Commander Craft I was just checking up on the flash of light close to our solar system that Kim Moon reported to us sir. And I did find something interesting. (Commander Craft) Oh really what's that Captain? (David) Well sir everything that Kim Moon said about not being any debris was correct but I did find high levels of radiation. Which could have come from a massive nuclear explosion. And there would probably be a flash of light that you could see for several light years away. Kim said it was a real bright flash. But the radiation might already have been there prior to the flash. Maybe reminisce of an exploding star. When we first seen the meteor on Earth and was tracking it. There was some talk because it changed directions twice and we tried to look at all-analytical possibilities. One of them was that it could be a spacecraft. So as we were tracking it on a certain heading and we seen a large flash of light and it vanished. Well farther down on that same heading about 1 light year away we seen another flash of light and then we did not see any more flashes of light until just now sir. The second flash of light was 3 minutes after the meteor disappeared. Which would have put the speed at approximately over 300,000 miles an hour. Now if you calculate time and speed from the second flash of light to the third flash of light. And David started using his calculator on his computer console and said the spacecraft would have to be going four times the speed of light sir. Although the third flash of light was on the same heading as our meteor. I don't see how it could be connected to the second flash of light because they are too far from each other. But it is technically an analytical possibility but only if that spacecraft has that kind of light speed capability. Capability of going four times the speed of light. It would have to have cloaking capability. Because in that particular area there is nothing anywhere in that region.

Hide and Seek

Chapter 13

I'll program my computer to sound and alert if it sees anything in that region out of the ordinary from this point on. (Commander Craft) Captain Braymer would you look way ahead of the last flash on the same heading? (David) Yes sir, that would be us sir. That heading is coming directly to our solar system toward Pluto sir.

Commander there does appear to be something, it appears to be a gas trail sir. Give me a minute sir and I'll tell you what kind of gas it is. (Commander) Sure Captain, take your time. (David) Here it is sir, it looks like it's a radioactive carbon trail and it's on that exact heading of the last reported heading of the meteor sir. And what the heck is this? Found it sir. Then David zoomed in. It appears to be a moon sir, and its parked right behind Pluto sir. It's not moving at all now either sir. (Commander). You're kidding me, right. (David) No sir, I'm not. (Commander) I'm reporting this to the Admiral. Are you sure Captain it's not Pluto's regular moon? (David) I'm positive sir, not only that Commander, but this moon has the same dimensions as the meteor we were tracking on Earth. Sir it's exactly ten kilometers in diameter. The meteor that was coming from the constellation of Scorpio was also ten kilometers in size. The odds of that are a million to one sir. Admiral this is Commander Craft sir. We have a situation here sir. We've been tracking a carbon trail from that last reported flash of light close to our solar system and we believe we've found a U.F.O. disguised as a moon behind Pluto sir. (Admiral Benson) Yes I know commander I have been watching everything from my office. Is everyone sure of their readings Commander? (Commander Craft) We'll check one more time sir. Captain please double check you readings one more time. (David) Yes sir, two minutes later. Sir our ship's computer has just completed its system check on my station and we are functioning at 100% accurate. (Commander Craft) Admiral we are done with our systems check, and we are operating at 100% accurate sir. (Admiral Benson) Commander I'm going to have to get back to you. I've got to make a phone call to Earth on this one. Let me report our findings and then we will have a briefing on this. (Commander Craft) Admiral one more question, should we go to yellow alert? (Admiral Benson) No Commander, we are real close but not yet if that moon starts moving go ahead and go yellow alert. I'll get back with you in a little while Commander. (Commander Craft) Yes sir. About an hour went by and Admiral Benson called back. Commander I'm setting up a briefing in my office in one hour. That will be 0330. (Commander Craft) Yes sir. (Admiral Benson) Commander we only need you, Captain Braymer, Lieutenant Fisher, and Commander Tice. (Commander Craft) Yes sir we'll see you in one hour. (Admiral Benson) Thank you Commander.

(Commander Craft) Yes sir. Ok listen up Captain Braymer, Commander Tice, Lieutenant Fisher we have a briefing in the Admirals office in one hour at 0330. Everyone said yes sir about the same time. As it got close to 0315 David didn't notice any change on the moon around Pluto so everyone started to get up and head to the Admirals Office. When they finally arrived everyone sat down in the Admirals office where there were already chairs set up. The Admiral stood up and started talking to Commander Craft for a minute. Then he started addressing everyone. Lady's and gentleman I have just receive new orders. We are to stop on our present course and to head to Pluto's moon to check out our new friends. They have been watching this down on Earth. Something else I wanted to talk to you about and that is how battle ready we are. All of us really do not have combat experience aboard the Lunar Base 1 and if these aliens are hostile. We could be in a lot of trouble. We don't know if our weapons will be affective. We do know how much more advanced they are from our ship. We only know they are. So there's a good chance that they have more powerful weapons. We have to be alert and know what we are doing in battle. Suppose for instance in battle we lose gravity. We would have to fight the battle without gravity.

Also this ship separates into three sections. We have never tried that yet either. I also want us to go watch the Lunar Base 1 battle ready training video at our stations, On stage separation also over and over before we go into battle. (David) Sir does each section have weapons capability. (Admiral Benson) Yes they do. Our section and the middle section also have a smaller engine on it for power. We would also have to separate before we approach the enemy. We may not get a second chance.

(David) I have one more question sir. (Admiral Benson) What's that Captain? (David) Well sir, I was wondering if we had any kind of shields sir, like on star trek? (Admiral Benson) Very good question Captain. The answer is yes we do. Our shields are all over on certain parts of the ship in vital areas on the outside. They are a liquid that turns into the strength of four inches of steel when it gets hard because of being exposed to the cold of space. They also have heaters on them to turn it back into a liquid state again. All of our windows have a thick peace of steel for shutter's that close when we go to red alert. (David) Wow that's impressive, thank you sir. (Admiral Benson) Any time Captain, that was a good question. Does that make everyone fill at ease? Everyone said yes sir. (Admiral Benson) I should have had the ship's doctor in on this briefing too. How's all of our weapons look Commander, are we battle ready. (Commander Craft) Yes sir. The only thing is, we have never tested them in battle. But all systems are operating at 100% sir. Also our five shuttles are in good operating condition. They're brand new and their weapons are ready to go sir. We need to put our pilots and shuttles and our clinics on standby and readiness. I will go brief the head doctor after we leave here sir. Then Admiral Benson called Lieutenant Parsons on the bridge. Lieutenant Parsons we need to change course and speed. Go ahead and plot a coarse to Pluto and raise our speed to mock seven. (Lieutenant parsons) Yes sir, I'm laying our new coarse and speed in now sir. (Admiral Benson) Thank you Lieutenant. We will all be joining you back on the bridge in a few minutes. We are going to practice our emergency protocols. (Lieutenant Parsons) Yes sir, we will be seeing you in a few minutes sir. (Admiral Benson) Ok Commander Tice you go brief Doctor King and I want everyone else to practice emergency procedures back on the bridge. When we do get back to the bridge, does everybody understand what all we will be doing? If not at your station on your computer, go to protocol and then go to your each individual station and it will tell you what your duties are and emergency procedure, to about any scenario. This briefing is officially over. Then everyone said, yes sir. (Admiral) Ok then let's all head back to the bridge and study. Everyone said yes sir, and headed back to the bridge. And on the way back you could tell David was thinking, "What did I get myself into". When everyone arrived at the bridge, they started practicing, and studying all of the emergency procedures including some combat strategies. They studied for a couple of hours. Then all of a sudden one of David's light's on his station console started to flash. David looked down and seen it and started to identify what it was. It was the Moon ship. It was on the move. (David) Admiral, our Moon friend is on the move. (Admiral Benson) Well here we go campers. Commander Tice go to yellow alert. (Commander Tice) Yes sir, going to yellow alert now sir. Suddenly the yellow light started flashing on the wall and you heard the navy whistle go off for five seconds and then it was just the flashing a yellow light again. (Admiral Benson) What direction is it headed Captain? (David) Sir, the Moon ship was going away from us slowly and then they changed course and speed and know it's coming directly at us at a high rate of speed sir. (Admiral Benson) Commander Tice, go to red alert and come to full stop and let's turn on and try them shields out. Put everything on the main viewer. This is one hell of a way to try everything out. Lets prepare for all three separations. Commander Craft you will need to go to the aft section and take charge and prepare for separation. Commander Tice you need to go take command of the middle section and prepare for separation. Remember gentleman we are on red alert. You have 15 minute to get there and get strapped in and to get situated. Lieutenant Courtney contact U.S.S. Lunar Base 2 and 3, and Earth and confer with them. Let's get a four-way conference call going Lieutenant.

(Lieutenant Courtney) Yes sir, a couple of minutes went by and Lieutenant Courtney said Admiral sir. The U.S.S. Lunar Base two is going to launch in ten minutes sir, they're going to position them self's between us, and Lunar Base 3 and Earth sir. Then they're going to separate and defend Earth in case we don't stop them sir.

Earth is launching more shuttles to dock with Lunar Base 3 sir. They are readying their ground missiles and their Laser's sir. (Admiral Benson) Good, It sounds like we've got a good plain. A few more minutes went by and first Commander Tice reported in and then

Commander Craft reported in. (Admiral Benson) Are we all about ready for separation? Both Commander Craft and Commander Tice said affirmative Admiral.

Then the Admiral said prepare for separation on my mark. Now go for full separation. All of a sudden we started to separate. Separation was going smoothly to everyone's surprise. (Captain Braymer) Admiral our alien Moon ship will be here in six minutes.

(Admiral Benson) Well Commanders lets warm up our engines and get in our half diamond defensive stance. And ready all weapons. Sir our alien guest's are slowing to stop. Commanders I hope all of your shields are up and operating.

Ok lets follow my lead Commanders. I'm going to try to communicate with them first. Our first alien contacts. (Lieutenant Courtney) Admiral, the Lunar Base 2 are almost into full separation sir. The Lunar Base 2 is now in position sir.

Our New Friends

Chapter 14

All of a sudden the alien ship was right in front of the Admiral's U.S.S Lunar Base One.

(Admiral Benson) Open a line to the alien ship Lieutenant with a nice greeting. (Lieutenant Courtney) What language sir?

(Admiral) Let's try English Lieutenant. (Lieutenant Courtney) Yes sir. There was a pause of about five minutes and then. Sir we are receiving a return message in English. (Admiral Benson) Put it on the COM Lieutenant. (Lieutenant Courtney) Yes sir. Hello people from Earth, we are on a peaceful mission of exploration for other life forms to make friends and trade only. We mean you no harm. We would like to meet with you and to get to know you better. Please do not be bothered by our appearance. (Admiral Benson) This is Admiral Benson of the U.S.S. Lunar Base 1. We had hoped this, because we would like the same thing very much too. Your appearance will not bother us and we mean you no harm. We just have a few questions for you. One was what were you doing around the planet Pluto, that is on the outskirts of our solar system. Are you the ship that was coming from the constellation of Scorpio? And one final question, what are you doing in our solar system. (Aliens) We did not want to frighten you so we were behind your planet Pluto observing you. We found that many planets get very frightened when we come directly to their home planet. Because of obvious reasons. We meant no harm. We have been watching you for a few of your years. We would like to be your friends.

We are like you in many ways but our appearance is different than yours. Our appearance does frighten some worlds. But we are not out to hurt anyone. We have also been monitoring your satellite communications and your television network. We like a lot of your movies to. We only want to have a peaceful friendship with you. And to exchange technologies and possibly do some trade. We come from the fourth planet from the star you call An tares in the constellation of Scorpio. We are on planets all over the universe and we do a lot of trade all over the galaxy. (Admiral Benson) Lunar Base 2 and 3 stand down to yellow alert. Lieutenant Parsons stand down to yellow alert. Well we are hoping we could get together with you, and celebrate with a good meal. So we could get to know one another a little better. We was also hoping you could send us some of your recipes and we will prepare a great feast for you. (Aliens) Thank you, Admiral that is very kind of you, we are honored. We will bring some of our recipes, but we will eat whatever you are eating. We look forward to trying your foods. If you want Admiral you could send a transport and we will bring it into our cargo bay doors with a tracking beam for safety. Then we will load onto your ship and come to you if that is all right.

(Admiral Benson) That's excellent sir, by the way what do we call your people? My ship is called in your language, the Galumpa which means in your language the Star Lion. Or Star king of the beast and my name in short is Captain Tudmoke. My people are called Powleens.(Admiral Benson) Excellent Captain, glad to meet you. We will send one of our shuttles to pick you up in about one hour and we will drop you off after we eat. (Captain Tudmoke) Very good Admiral, we will see you then. (Admiral Benson) I look forward to dinning with you Captain Tudmoke. The Admiral finished his communiqué with Captain Tudmoke. Everyone was looking at each other with a kind of funny look. The Admiral said well that could not have gone any better. Captain Braymer I'm going to my office and you are in charge of the bridge. Lieutenant Courtney when I get to my office I want you to patch all of the communications with Lunar Base 2 and 3 and the Earth to my office. I will be there in three minutes. I will let you know when I'm ready. Thank you. (Lieutenant Courtney) Yes sir. (Admiral Benson) Captain Braymer, stay on yellow alert unless I tell you different. And keep them shields on. (David) Yes sir. David started thinking, wow I've been at work for 48 hours and I'm already in charge of the ship. I wonder what tomorrow is going to bring. Three minutes went by and like clock work, the Admiral contacted the bridge and had the calls transferred to him. The Admiral started talking with the President of the United States. Well Mr. President what do you think about our current situation. Admiral I just want to say what a great job your doing. We are all watching you down here on Earth. You're on every channel. I would like you to continue on what you just set up. I could not have done a better job than you just did Admiral. Go ahead and have your dinner and get to know our new friends. The whole world can't wait to see what our new friends look like. We will be watching from down here. We'll know more after your dinner and we'll have another conference afterwards. So once again keep up the good work. Admiral Benson I would also like to give my first combat promotion. Admiral I'm making you Admiral of our space fleet. You're the head of all the base stations and anything else that's in space in this solar system. (Admiral Benson) Thank you sir. I don't know what to say.

(The President) No, thank you Admiral. Just keep up the great work your doing Admiral. You should have seen it from down here on Earth Admiral. It was live on all the networks. When you and Lunar Base 2 separated and when you went to red alert just like on T.V. it was unbelievable. And when the alien spaceship parked right in front of you, I truly believe you could of heard a pin drop anywhere on Earth. It was historical Admiral to say the least. Also I wanted to tell you whatever you do don't pick a fight with our new friends.

You have done a perfect job up till now. We're counting on you Admiral. (Admiral Benson) Thank you sir. (The President) No, thank you sir. Good luck Admiral. The President hung up his phone and the Admiral headed back to the bridge. When the Admiral arrived back at the bridge he told Lieutenant Courtney to call the docking bay and ready the shuttle and to set up our dinner right there by the landing bay in the briefing room. Contact the kitchen and go ahead and start setting that up. (Lieutenant Courtney) Admiral sir, the kitchen called about a minute before you arrived and they want to know what they should prepare for dinner sir. (Admiral Benson) What's our choice's Lieutenant. Well sir we have just about everything here as we do on Earth. So may I recommend, why don't we have a couple of vegetarian meals and a couple of meat entree's sir. (Admiral Benson) Very good Lieutenant, you know I was just thinking maybe we should not serve any meat. We can have it ready in case they ask for it. But only if they ask for it. Ok Lieutenant? (Lieutenant Courtney) Yes sir. (Admiral Benson) Also Lieutenant contact Commander Tice on his ship section and tell him to have a security team close by but totally out of view when we have our dinner.

Also tell Commander Tice to send the shuttle in fifteen minutes. One more thing, I want everyone on there nicest behavior at this dinner. Also Commander Craft stay alert and your in charge of operations while Captain Braymer and myself, and also Commander Tice, Doctor King, also I want a couple of our largest security in full dress to join us. In fact I want all of us in full dress uniforms. Ok, everyone I just listed is dismissed to go get in full dress uniforms. We will meet down in the cargo bay areas where they have set up dinner with our new friends.

Also Lieutenant call Commander Tice and tell him to get in full dress uniforms and join the diner. I want him to supervise the shuttle mission to pick up our friends to attend our dinner. We have to look good because I'm told everyone is watching us down on Earth. (Lieutenant Courtney) Yes sir, (Admiral Benson) Well Lieutenant Parsons she's your bridge now. You can watch us at our dinner on your screen. We should know more by the end of dinner. Like what our next move will be. I can't wait to see what these aliens look like. (Lieutenant Parsons) I know sir. I can't wait to see myself. Sir Commander Tice just launched in the shuttle to the alien ship. (Admiral Benson) Ok Lieutenant, I've got to go get in full dress. Take over. (Lieutenant Parsons) Yes sir. Good luck sir. (Admiral Benson) Thank you Lieutenant we're going to need it. The Admiral hurried away to get dressed. When David got back to his place he called Lieutenant Heather Courtney the young lady that helped him when he first arrived to help him with his full dress uniform. David did not know that much about it. After the Lieutenant told David what to wear and how to arrange his uniform correctly. David thanked her and he hurried to the cargo bay area. The Lieutenant gave him directions. When David finally arrived everyone else was just arriving also. Everybody started talking and wondering what our new friends looked like. Then all of a sudden the shuttle started its journey back to the Lunar Base 1 from the alien spaceship. You could hear the shuttles pilot talking. Lunar Base 1 this is Warrant Officer Steven Davis of the shuttle wonderer, requesting permission to dock? Roger that, this is Lunar Base 1, permission granted. Prepare to dock. (The Shuttle Wonderer) Lunar Base 1 our computer is locked on and we are in docking mode.

The shuttle wonderer docked without a problem. Everyone waited in anticipation to see the aliens. Then everyone started to unload. As our alien friends were unloading they came out one at a time. They looked humanoid, they were way taller than us. I would say about seven foot tall and there face was rough looking almost as if they were burnt. Their skin color was a three tone of a light brown and they had very little visible hair but what hair they did have looked like thin black wire. They were muscular built but had a slender side to them. Their arms and legs and torso looked elongated. There were five of them. Their Captain Tudmoke was the first to unload and then his crew. Admiral Benson greeted Captain Tudmoke and escorted them to the room where they had everything set up for their meal. The sitting arrangements were set up in the typical round table style. On one side of the table there was Admiral Benson and Commander

Tice, then Captain Braymer, Doctor King and two of our biggest security officers we had. On the other side Captain Tudmoke and his men. (Admiral Benson) This is such a great honor for us at this historical meeting. We are sorry if you don't like our food. We didn't really know what to serve so we put a little bit of everything out. If you have any questions just ask. We hope you like it. (Captain Tudmoke) Thank you Admiral for your extra consideration. We eat about the same things you do. We have been watching your television for about fifty of your years. A lot of our little animals are similar to yours. We are like you in many ways. For instance some of us eat some meats and some of us don't. We also have been monitoring your construction of your base stations and we are very impressed. My ship is one of our best star cruisers. We have about 2,000 other ships not all of them like mine.

My ship at present has 25,000 crewmen on board. The Galumpa can hold up to 35,000 crew if needed. Some of the other ships are similar to mine and some are cargo transports. Some are privately owned. We have ships all over the universe. But we only have one ship in your solar system. Admiral if you want us to leave. We will leave without any problems. (Admiral Benson) Oh no sir. We are honored to have you here. And we like what we see. We want to get to know you better to, as long as there's no conflict. We're happy. (Captain Tudmoke) Excellent Admiral. There shouldn't be any conflict on our part. We fill exactly the same way as you. We would also like to start with the trading of our two worlds products and produce. We also trade with many other worlds and we trade their goods too. (Admiral Benson) We would love to do this with you. We look forward to being good friends and neighbors. Our world and the one's we deal with has many different products and many types of produce we would love to trade with you. (Admiral Benson) As Admiral of our space fleet I am particularly interested in your ship and its engines. We would love to know about any other worlds and their people and some of your adventures out in the universe. This kind of stuff fascinates our people on Earth.

I think because we are mainly people who like to explore the unknown for the good of all and ultimate knowledge. We truly love to meet new people from other worlds and trade with them as long as there's no conflicting problem. In fact it's are dream. Then Captain Tudmoke said, we will be more than happy to show you or exchange some of our technologies too. But you have to understand that if we give you some type of our technology and you used it to control your planet. We would be in trouble from our superiors.

But we could possibly work out some kind of deal. We want to also thank you for this great meal. What exactly is this here? (David) That's a vegetable we call asparagus. One of my favorites too. If you like asparagus then I bet you'll like to try some of these. We call this a baked potato. We stir it up into a soft pudding and then we add butter and salt. Potatoes also grow well in space. I hope you will like it. (Captain Tudmoke) I believe I will try it. MMM that's good. We have something like this on our planet its called stemage. What is this food here, it sure is good, Lieutenant Dogmas one of Captains Tudmoke officers asked? (Admiral Benson) That is what we call a desert on Earth. We usually eat our desert after we eat our main meal.

That particularly desert is called chocolate ice cream. Captain how did your people learn our English language so well? (Captain Tudmoke) Like I said earlier, we have been watching your planet for a number of years. Myself and all of my officers had to learn your language for this mission. We were going to come, back in 2008 but there was too much conflict going on in your world. We debated it for a long time whether it would have stop the fighting on your world at the time by showing up but sometimes we get the opposite reaction when we show up on the scene because of fear. So we try to wait for a peaceful moment in time when we make first contact. We were like you in your current technological state about two hundred of your years ago. Since then we have developed light speed and we have colonized hundreds of worlds all over the universe. And we do not mind sharing our technology with you as long as you do not hurt anyone with it. Or try to control other planets. We cannot allow that to happen. If you did do this we would fill responsible and we would have to stop you.

(Admiral Benson) We understand your position and we assure you that we would not do this. We are a peaceful people more or less. And we would only fight in a defensive posture. We are not out to control anyone. We are only looking for friends for trade of goods and technology. We try to do as fair of a deal as possible when we do trade. (Captain Tudmoke) Admiral if you would like a tour of my ship we have one of our rooms set up to look at some of the products that we trade throughout the universe. We also have like a museum of artifacts from other worlds if you would like to join us after our historically wonderful meal. If you want you can bring some of your crew with you. (Admiral Benson) We would love to tour your ship, it would be a great honor sir. If you would like I will take you on a tour of our ship after the meal and then we'll all go to your ship. We were all so impressed with the size of your ship and its speed. It is bigger than anything we have. (Captain Tudmoke) Our ship is, how do you say ten kilometers in diameter. You know Admiral I have wanted to tell you, that just as your entire world is watching this on your satellite television so is my world using your satellites.

Hydra The Dragon

Chapter 15

This is also a historical event on my planet. My planet is called Sybon and it is a cross between your Earth and your Jupiter mixed and my people are called Powleens and we've wanted to have first contact with you for many years. In fact there has been many debates on this issue on my planet also for many years. We just want to make new friends and do our trade. Through trade we progress and prosper on our world. We have trade on many worlds throughout the universe. We try to offer are technology for goods too. We also have many products and produce we trade from our world and many others. Just like we like your asparagus and potatoes. I believe you're going to like a lot of our products. We have many products that are loved on many worlds throughout the stars. There are many new healing food products. A lot of advances in Health-care also. (Admiral Benson) This all sounds great to us we would love to not only be friends with you, but we would love to start trading for some of your goods. We will give you some of our catalogs of our many products to take back to your ship to look over. Also Captain Tudmoke I would like to talk to you about communications. You seem to know how our communications work but we do not know anything about yours like for instance if we could communicate ship to ship on our video monitoring system it would be a lot better. (Captain Tudmoke) Yes Admiral, our computers are capable of this but we make sure that we don't inadvertently download any type of harmful viruses onto our system. Something that might work ok for your computer system may not be all right for our computer system or the other way around. We can contact you right now by Video but you cannot contact us. If you would like I'll have our systems expert and yours look at your computer system to see if it would hurt our system or your system. You know just to see if they are compatible. And if it checks out, I don't see why we couldn't hook up to our computer video communications. (Admiral Benson) That's excellent Captain Tudmoke. I have one more question I would like to ask you. Is there any anti social alien races out there that might be harmful to our world that we need to know about? (Captain Tudmoke) That is a very good question Admiral. Yes there are some alien worlds that are not very friendly out there. We are presently having trouble with two other worlds that are connected to each other in the same solar system. All we did was try to set up some friendly trade with them and they seemed to fear us and they turned on us for trespassing. They said we were trying to invade them. We weren't, we were just trying to do the same thing as we are doing here now with you. We have had several confrontations with them. They are called the Arcons and their friends are called Thracians. They don't have light speed capability like we do yet but they are almost there. I fill that we are a little more advanced than them but they don't think so. They do have some pretty advanced weaponry however. But believe it or not even primitive weapons can be very affective in space. They have problems with more than one world. We are not an aggressive world if we feel there's going to be a problem, we usually try to honor your wishes and leave. But we were attacked more than once by the Arcons and we had to defend ourselves and they lost a couple of ships that they are a little resentful about, but it was in self-defense. We still do not want trouble with them so we mainly stay away from their solar system. The Arcons are the third planet from the star you call Gamma Hydra from the constellation of Hydra, the Dragon. The Thracians are the second planet from the star Gamma Hydra. They have been leaving their solar system a lot more than usual lately. Both of them together do not have half as many ships as we do. We have had several cargo ships destroyed that we are currently investigating in a couple of different systems. And there have been a couple of sightings of Arcon ships in the area. I don't think that you have anything to worry about here. Especially now that we are friends. They probably already know about you but there is a chance they don't. You do have a beautiful world and it does seem to stand out and is very visible in space. We saw it very clearly. And I know if we seen it they probably did too. (Admiral Benson) Well, not only has this been an historical Day but we have met some great new neighbors too and it has been very educational. Why don't we finish our meal and we will talk along the way as we take you on the tour of our ship. Then we will go to your ship for your tour and then we will convey what we have learned to our superiors. We'll exchange information and set up everything from there. How's that sound Captain. (Captain Tudmoke) That sounds good Admiral. By the way what kind of food is this? (Captain Braymer) That's what we call eggplant parmesan. (Captain Tudmoke) This is very good. Then Admiral Benson said, that's one of my favorite too Captain. Everyone finished eating and went on their tour of the Lunar Base 1. As they were checking everything out Captain Tudmoke commented on how impressed he was especially when the Lunar Base 1 split into three different ships all independent of each other. Even David learned a lot more about his ship. Then everyone loaded upon the shuttle Wonderer to go to the Powleens ship. Everyone was very excited about going on the alien space ship. As they left the docking bay on the Lunar Base 1 Captain Tudmoke's ship grabbed them with their tracking beam. Then they pulled us right into their cargo bay and set us down like we were a baby. The inside of the alien ship looked similar to ours but the rooms were much higher and bigger probably because of their height. They had an average height of about seven foot tall. You could tell that they had a large crew. What everyone couldn't get over was that their ship was as big as a small moon. It was ten kilometers in diameter. It was enormous. You could walk all day long and still not see everything. Their elevator was like a train car that went all over the ship. It wasn't slow either. The first place they took us was probably the most interesting of all. It was the museum that they had. It was as big as a four story building. Each exhibit that they had of different alien races was set up in its own room. They had hundreds of different alien exhibits. They had aliens from all over the universe. There were some very odd-looking aliens and some pretty scary looking characters. One of the Admirals crew, one of the security officers was videoing the whole tour. (Admiral Benson) Captain Tudmoke your ship the Galumpa is incredible, it's so big! And your museum is nothing short of remarkable. We want to thank you again for allowing us to see all of your ship and for visiting us. We are so very happy to be your friends, and so glad you came to us today. (Captain Tudmoke) Admiral, it's our pleasure to be here. I only wish we had done it a long time ago. But you know if we had came a long time ago who knows how it might of turned out. Look what happened to us with the Arcons. Also Admiral we have ships for sell or trade that are very advanced from your own. (Admiral Benson) We would like to do a lot of trade with you now if you would like. I'll just tell my superiors and we'll work all of the details out. Then they all walked in the next exhibit. It was their anti social friends they were talking about, the Arcons and in the room next to the Arcons was the Thracians. Arcons were humanoid but they looked like they were part snake and part human together. The Thracians looked like they were humanoid too and some kind of a mammal mix, they had big Dog like teeth. The Thracians were also very tall and muscular. They were even bigger than the Powleens. They didn't have the slender look like the Powleens either. They just looked like they were solid mussel. They were giants about eight foot tall. The Arcons were our size but they were scary looking. We could not understand the writing that was on each exhibit but the models and pictures were self-explanatory. Captain Dopar explained to us that the Arcons would bite their victims to make them sleep, then devour them whole. The Arcons and Thracians were some terrifying looking aliens.

They showed what each world looked like in a small hologram and what their ships looked like and there hand held weapons and even some of the plants and animals on their planets. After the long tour nobody was bored. Everyone seemed like they were in a state of fascination. As everyone was loading back onto the shuttle to go back, the Admiral and Captain Tudmoke were talking about an exchange of a couple of crewman for a couple of days to go over everything and to talk about trading technology's and products. We left one of the security officers and Commander Tice and we got a couple of their crewman and headed back to our ship. As they arrived back, the Admiral instructed Lieutenant Heather Courtney to set up quarters for their new guest and said he was heading to his office and for everyone to go back to their stations and that he would join them in a little while. He also said to go ahead and stand down from yellow alert. The Admiral hurried to his office to talk to the President and to update him on all that has transpired. He got through pretty easy because the President was waiting with anticipation. (The President)

Well Admiral how did it go on the alien ship. I bet you have a lot to tell. (Admiral Benson) Yes sir I do, Well sir first I would like to say we are on the verge of going into another era. Talks went great sir. (The President) Thank God Admiral. I was hoping you were going to say that. Now I know I picked the right man for the job. I'm sorry to interrupt Admiral please tell me more? (Admiral Benson) Yes sir, the Powleens are a very civilized and very advanced people. They are willing to sell or trade their space ships and technology and anything else that we are interested in. They seem to just be interested in making new friends and doing a lot of trade.

I believe they are being honest sir. On our tour we had seen a lot in their museum. We seen and learned about other life forms all over the universe.

Star Wars

Chapter 16

Some are in the constellation of Gamma Hydra the Dragon that are not so friendly called the Arcons and the Thracians. Two inhabited different worlds close to the star called Gamma Hydra we need to watch for. They let us video the whole tour and we will send a copy directly to you as soon as I go back to the bridge sir. Also Mr. President I fill we should try to move on these trade deals with the Powleens especially on the trade of their spacecrafts sir we could advance in light speed space travel over night. I would like to start with negotiations as soon as possible. Sir I can't emphasize enough about how we need to get to know these people better. This is a match made in heaven sir. (The President) You know Admiral you have done a tremendous job here. I could not have done it any better myself. Also Admiral I wonder if we might be able to start any planetary exchange of people. They could leave some here and we could send some back with them? (Admiral Benson) One more thing sir. Captain Tudmoke was telling me that just as everyone on Earth is watching this historical advent so is their planet. The Powleens are taping in on our satellites and have been watching us on their T.V. and have been for about fifty years sir. Also sir I feel if they wanted to they could have swatted us like flies. But they didn't. Instead they treated us with kindness. They are way advanced of us. That's why I think their legit sir. I will talk to them about the exchange of personnel from world to world. Now do we have them move forward to Earth or do we keep them out here for a little while longer sir? (The President) Lets keep them out there a little bit longer maybe a day or two more Admiral. Just keep on doing what you're doing Admiral. You guys may have to work a little over time but it's for the good of mankind. You know Admiral I didn't expect this in a million years. As a politician I'm at a loss for words, and you don't see that much. We need to appoint committees on what questions to ask our new friends. (Admiral Benson) Well sir I guess that about covers everything so I will head back to the bridge and get started. (The President) Very Good Admiral, good luck. Thank you sir, end communiqué the Admiral said and then headed back to the bridge. As he arrives back at the bridge he notices everyone was talking and so excited about our new friends. Admiral Benson told Lieutenant Courtney to send a copy of the video of the tour we took onboard the Powleens ship to the President as soon as its ready. (Lieutenant Courtney) Yes sir right away. (Admiral Benson) Well Captain are you glad you signed on? (Captain Braymer) Oh yes sir, I've seen so much in the last two days, it all seems like a dream or a fantasy. Sometimes it all does not seem real sir. I still haven't even unpacked any of my stuff yet. But you know everything is so exciting I don't even care. I'm just now starting to familiarize myself with my station. (Admiral Benson) Captain I was wondering if you mind sharing your station with one of our new guest when they come up to the bridge. (David) Not at all sir, After all I am the 1st Science Officer. I find it very interesting sir. I also thought their ship was incredible. (Admiral Benson) Yes I know as an Admiral of a fleet it was like I was a kid in a candy store. I can't wait to get some of their ships. Then the Powleens and Lieutenant Fisher came in through the bridge door. (David) Hello Officer Benish. Your place will be right over here next to me. I will show you everything. Then his computer started to flash a red light. Wait what's this? Sir I am picking something up on my computer scan of our outer solar system. Hmmm, but sir when I try to isolate it, it shows nothing. It shows something going about 150,000 miles an hour. It could be another cloaked ship sir. It appears to be coming this way sir. (Admiral Benson) Captain what is it you do see that makes you think there's something there? (David) Sir my computer is saying there seems to be a radioactive dust trail. (Admiral Benson) Lieutenant Parsons put the location of the ship on full screen and go to yellow alert. (Lieutenant Parsons) Yes sir. (Admiral Benson) I don't see anything at all there. Lieutenant Courtney contact the Powleens and ask them if they have any more ships headed this way and also ask them if they see our dust trail. (Lieutenant Courtney) Yes sir. (Admiral Benson) Captain Braymer, keep an eye on our new friend and can you give me an estimated time of arrival on this incoming ship. (David) Yes sir. (Lieutenant Courtney) Sir, the Powleens are going to battle stations. They believe we are getting ready to meet our other neighbors the Arcons. They also recommend that we let them handle the Arcons. (David) Admiral our guest will be here in sixteen minutes sir.

(Admiral Benson) Lieutenant Parsons when that ship gets half way to us I want you to go to red alert. (Lieutenant Parsons) Yes sir. (Admiral Benson) Lieutenant Courtney I want you to acknowledge to the Powleens that we give them permission to confront the Arcons but we prefer to do it without violence if possible and if a conflict does happen to tell the Arcons that we are not involved with this dispute. We will fire back if someone fires on us but we do not wish to fight them. We are a friendly world. Also contact Earth and the other two base station's and brief them on what's going on. (Lieutenant Courtney) Yes sir. (David) Sir, The Powleens are firing up their engines and they're starting to pull away. Also, Admiral their ship is giving off a lot of radiation too. About 500 Rankin's per sq foot sir. And suddenly the Powleens ship started picking up speed. After they were far enough away you seen a flash of light and then they just disappeared. (David) Admiral that sure is breath taking sir. (Admiral Benson) Captain all I keep on thinking about is I hope nothing is going to hurt our arrangement with the Powleens. Just like you said earlier we have come centuries ahead in just a couple of days. There have been so many new doors that are opening up to Earth and proof of other intelligent life forms. Unbelievable. That's why I'm considering helping the Powleens if they need it. (David) Sir, there was just another flash of light. It appears that the Powleens have position themselves between them and us. Sir the Powleens are 50,000,000 miles away from us now. It took them eight minutes and 46 seconds. Sir it appears that the Powleens put themselves out of our reach, maybe on purpose. Sir we couldn't get there if we wanted to. (Admiral Benson) Wow, that s unbelievable. Ok Lieutenant Parsons will you zoom the Galumpa in on the main viewer?

All this is just remarkable. (David) Admiral, you're not going to believe this. There are three more radiation trails coming towards us at a high rate of speed right behind the first one sir. They are coming from the constellation of Hydra the Dragon. (Admiral Benson) Now this is not looking so good. What are we going to do? (Lieutenant Courtney) Sir you are getting a communiqués from Earth. It's the President sir. He is saying he does not want us to engage the Arcons under any circumstance. Unless we are attacked first. (David) Sir, the Arcons ship is just about to arrive at the Powleens position and there are three more ships on the way. Sir the Arcon ship just turned visible. And right when he said that. The Arcon ship became visible on the main viewer. Then it came to a stop right in front of the Powleens ship. Time was starting to go by and the Admiral said I wish I could hear what was being said. The whole crew looked like they were filled with uncertainty and curiosity. And all of a sudden the Arcon ship started attacking the Powleens ship with what looked like a red pulse weapon and it was slamming the Galumpa repeatedly. Then it looked like the Galumpa opened up with everything they had. The Galumpa was so huge. It had weapons all over it. You could see a bombardment of fire onto the Arcon ship. Both ships were taking a barrage of multiple hits but they seemed to be handling it pretty good. The Arcon ship seem to have some kind of blue magnetic field for their shields and they were working pretty good. The Arcon ship wasn't near as big as the Powleens ship. It was about as big as our ship. It looked like the Powleens fire wasn't doing anything to the Arcons ship though. You could tell that the Powleens ship was getting hurt a little bit, because every now and then you could see some little piece of debris flying off. The pulse weapon was pretty strong looking. They just wouldn't stop hammering each other. Then suddenly Lieutenant Courtney said sir I just received a message from NASA that there were about forty flashes of light coming from all around our solar system region. (David) Sir the other three Arcon ships are just about to arrive at the battle scene. You should start to see them any second on the main viewer. Suddenly you could see all of the Arcon ships declock. There they are. Then the other three Arcon ships started slamming the Powleens ship with their pulse weapons. The Galumpa just kept taking it and firing all their weapons right back at the four Arcon ships and all of a sudden the first Arcon ship started losing its shields and then it exploded. Everybody on the Lunar Base 1 was cheering. Then you could tell the Galumpa was getting hurt worse because of bigger chunks of their ship was blasting off from the constant hammering of the pulse weapons from the other three Arcon ships. The Galumpa would just keep rotating the ship away from the damaged area's. Because it was round it worked really well. But it still did not look too good for the Galumpa. Suddenly one of the Arcon ships veered off of the Galumpa and started coming toward the Lunar Base 1. (David) Sir, one of the Arcon ships has veered off the Galumpa and is starting to come toward us. (Admiral Benson) Ok people here we go. Lets get battle ready. Red alert. Lieutenant fisher are you ready on our weapons? (Lieutenant Fisher) Yes sir, what would you like to be your primary weapon sir? (Admiral Benson) I would like the laser first but have our stinger rockets and our small arms fire on stand-by and if that doesn't work get ready to fire all weapons ok Lieutenant. If we are going to break through their shields it will probably be our Laser.

Lieutenant Courtney get ready to send a message in English to the Arcons. In the message tell them that we are peaceful and we do not wish to fight them. Also tell them that this dispute is between the Powleens and the Arcons not us. Go ahead and send the message now Lieutenant. (Lieutenant Courtney) Yes sir. You could see the Arcon ship. It was still steadily coming towards the Lunar Base 1. Also Lieutenant Courtney, send a message to our other two ships to be battle ready for when the Arcons arrive and wait for my order to fire. Man this sure is the hard way to test these shields.

The New Age

Chapter 17

Then the Arcon ship started to arrive. It started getting closer and then it slowed and finally stopped right in front of the middle section, dead center of all three ships. It wasn't as big as the Powleens ship but it was still big enough. It was as big as our ship. It was shaped like a single wing that was curled downward on each end of the wing with a bulge on top and bottom in the middle. Then before long we started to receive a message back. (Lieutenant Courtney) Sir we are receiving a message and the computer and I do not understand the language. What would you like me to do? (Admiral Benson) Let's just pick about three different languages and just keep repeating the same message Lieutenant. Then without any reason the Arcons open fired with their pulse weapons on all three-ship sections, and it was powerful. You could fill the pounding on our ship. It felt massive. Every time it hit us it seemed like the ship moved backwards about ten feet in space. But our shields held strong.

Then Admiral Benson said open fire with the lasers Lieutenant Parsons and the other two Lunar Base ship sections opened fired. You could see the three lasers all firing on the Arcon ship but it didn't seem to be hurting the Arcons but our shields were still holding too. Then Admiral Benson said, fire all weapons at will. Then everyone was firing everything they had. It was unbelievable. The Arcons weapons were pounding us. They seemed to be focusing more on Commander Crafts ship section but to our amazement the shields were holding. Then the shields started to give on Commander Crafts ship and just then it started taking a lot of damage but he just kept firing his weapons. Then finally the Arcons ship started to lose their shields and then all of a sudden it just exploded. The explosion was so great it push all three ship sections back about two miles in space but their shields held. Then everyone shouted yeaaaa! (Admiral Benson) Lieutenant Courtney get me a status report from Commander Craft and Commander Tices ship sections. I need to know how many casualties they have. Also get me a status report on our ship section Lieutenant. (Lieutenant Courtney) Yes sir. Suddenly there was a massive explosion on the Galumpa. It looked like the Arcons blew away a quarter section of the Galumpa. It started to drift and the Galumpa stopped using its weapons. The other Arcon ships just kept slamming the Galumpa with a barrage of their weapons. It looked like the end of the Galumpa. Then there were about forty flashes of light all around the battle scene. It was a whole fleet of Powleen ships of all different sizes and then the Arcons stopped firing on the Galumpa. The Arcon ship started to move over to their other ship that was drifting and then the Powleens started to open fire on the Arcons all at once on the two remaining ships.

The Arcon ship that was drifting even started to fire. And suddenly it exploded. Then one of the last two ships started to lose its shield and then it started drifting and it stopped firing. The Powleens stopped firing on the ship that was drifting. Finally the last Arcon ship started losing its shield but it was still firing so the Powleens just kept pounding it with multiple firing until it finally exploded in one big ball of fire. Everyone on Lunar Base 1 started to yell, cheer and applauded loudly and so did Earth. Then one of the Powleens ships went close to the remaining Arcon ship and grabbed it with their tractor beam and one after another flashed and then disappeared. When they got down to the last two ships one of them went over by the Galumpa and grabbed it with their tractor beam and then a flash of light and it was gone. Finally the last ship flashed and it was gone. (Lieutenant Courtney) Admiral the status report on the other two ships sections are ready sir. Commander Tices ship reported no damage and no casualties. Commander Crafts ship reports no casualties, some minor injuries though, a couple of bumps and bruises, and one broking arm sir. Damage wise they lost their main port shields but they didn't breach the hull, they almost did though sir. And our ship section received no Injuries and no damages sir. (Admiral Benson) Well we sure came out better than I thought we were. God must have been helping us on this one. (Lieutenant Fisher) Admiral I hope they didn't think that we didn't want to help them. (Admiral Benson) No Lieutenant I don't think that's it at all. They knew we were out of range. They are also watching us on their televisions on their home planet. They know we couldn't help them. (David) Admiral there's a radiation trail coming right toward us. Then suddenly the Powleen ship appeared in front of the Lunar Base 1. Captain Tudmoke came on the main viewer. Hello Admiral I hope everyone is all right. We are sorry that happened to you, we did not want that to happen. We tried not to fight but they were still mad about the first two of their ships that got destroyed the last time we met and they open fired on us, we had no choice but to defend ourselves. We also told them that this had nothing to do with Earth or anyone in this solar system. We also said that you were totally innocent in this and that you didn't even know who they were. Don't worry we won't abandon you if they come back to do harm to you. Remember we are monitoring your satellites and we will know if they come back and we also watch the stars pretty good to. Admiral Benson stood up in his place and said that battle was incredible sir. I hope you did not have many casualties and your ship the Galumpa is ok. We all applauded you sir. We are so glad you won the battle and are all right. It got pretty hairy there for a moment. We thought you were done for until your fleet came to the rescue. (Captain Tudmoke) Yes we did have a lot of casualties on the Galumpa. We almost were destroyed. We seen you had some trouble to Admiral. Your ships were very impressive, especially that laser of yours. You also won your first space battle. All of you did a great job. We thank you for your help. If the Arcon ship hadn't broke off and come to attack you we would have probably been destroyed. (Admiral Benson) No thank you sir, we had no casualties and we needed to check all of our equipment out anyway. We know you were totally innocent because we were watching. We are so happy for you too Captain. That was a great battle. We are sorry for all of your casualties though. We hope everything is still on with us. We are so sorry we couldn't have helped you more.

We wanted too. But we knew we couldn't make it to you in time. We don't have that kind of speed capability like you do. We also want to thank you for protecting our world. They could have done a lot of damage to us and now maybe they respect us a little. We also thank you from the bottom of our hearts for that. We hope that we can become good friends in the future. (Captain Tudmoke) I know we will be. It's in the stars Admiral. And don't worry we will take care of that speed problem with your spacecrafts. Our world's that day joined into a friendship that was pure gold. And Earth moved into a new age, when space travel launches us into the "Age of Aquarius".

The End

Printed in Great Britain
by Amazon.co.uk, Ltd.,
Marston Gate.